ELIZABETH GILL
CRIME DE LUXE

ELIZABETH GILL was born Elizabeth Joyce Copping in 1901, into a family including journalists, novelists and illustrators. She married for the first time, at the age of 19, to archaeologist Kenneth Codrington. Her second marriage, to artist Colin Gill, lasted until her death, at the age of only 32, in 1934, following complications from surgery.

She is the author of three golden age mystery novels, *The Crime Coast* (aka *Strange Holiday*) (1931), *What Dread Hand?* (1932), and *Crime de Luxe* (1933), all featuring eccentric but perceptive artist-detective Benvenuto Brown.

By Elizabeth Gill

ELIZABETH GILL

CRIME DE LUXE

With an introduction
by Curtis Evans

DEAN STREET PRESS

Published by Dean Street Press 2017

Copyright © 1933 Elizabeth Gill

Introduction copyright © 2017 Curtis Evans

All Rights Reserved

First published in 1933 by Cassell & Co.

Cover by DSP

ISBN 978 1 911579 23 6

www.deanstreetpress.co.uk

INTRODUCTION

THE DEATH OF Elizabeth Joyce Copping Gill on 18 June 1934 in London at the age of 32 cruelly deprived Golden Age detective fiction readers of a rapidly rising talent in the mystery fiction field, "Elizabeth Gill." Under this name Gill had published, in both the UK and the US, a trio of acclaimed detective novels, all of which were headlined by her memorably-named amateur detective, the cosmopolitan English artist Benvenuto Brown: *Strange Holiday* (in the US, *The Crime Coast*) (1929), *What Dread Hand?* (1932) and *Crime De Luxe* (1933). Graced with keen social observation, interesting characters, quicksilver wit and lively and intriguing plots, the three Benvenuto Brown detective novels are worthy representatives of the so-called "manners" school of British mystery that was being richly developed in the 1930s not only by Elizabeth Gill before her untimely death, but by the famed British Crime Queens Dorothy L. Sayers, Margery Allingham and Ngaio Marsh, as well as such lately rediscovered doyennes of detective fiction (all, like Elizabeth Gill, reprinted by Dean Street Press) as Ianthe Jerrold, Molly Thynne and Harriet Rutland.

Like her contemporaries Ianthe Jerrold and Molly Thynne, the estimable Elizabeth Gill sprang from a lineage of literary and artistic distinction. She was born Elizabeth Joyce Copping on 2 November 1901 in Sevenoaks, Kent, not far from London, the elder child of illustrator Harold Copping and his second wife, Edith Louisa Mothersill, daughter of a commercial traveler in photographic equipment. Elizabeth--who was known by her second name, Joyce (to avoid confusion I will continue to call her Elizabeth in this introduction)--was raised at "The Studio" in the nearby village of Shoreham, where she resided in 1911 with only her parents and a young Irish governess. From her father's previous marriage, Elizabeth had two significantly older half-brothers, Ernest Noel, who migrated to Canada before the Great War, and Romney, who died in 1910, when Elizabeth was but eight years old. Elizabeth's half-sister, Violet, had passed away in infancy before Elizabeth's birth, and a much younger brother, John Clarence, would be born to her parents in 1914. For much of her life, it seems, young Elizabeth essentially lived as an only child. Whether she was instructed privately or institutionally in the later years of her adolescence is unknown to me, but judging from her novels her education in the liberal arts must have been a good one.

Elizabeth's father Harold Copping (1863-1932) was the elder son of Edward Copping--a longtime editor of the *London Daily News* and the author of *The Home at Rosefield* (1861), a triple-decker tragic Victorian novel vigorously and lengthily denounced for its "morbid exaggeration of false sentiment" by the *Spectator* (26 October 1861, 24)—and Rose Heathilla Prout, daughter of watercolorist John Skinner Prout. Harold Copping's brother, Arthur E. Copping (1865-1941), was a journalist, travel writer, comic novelist and devoted member of the Salvation Army. Harold Copping himself was best-known for his Biblical illustrations, especially "The Hope of the World" (1915), a depiction of a beatific Jesus Christ surrounded by a multi-racial group of children from different continents that became an iconic image in British Sunday Schools; and the pieces collected in what became known as *The Copping Bible* (1910), a bestseller in Britain. Harold Copping also did illustrations for non-Biblical works, including such classics from Anglo-American literature as *David Copperfield*, *A Christmas Carol*, *Little Women* and *Westward, Ho!* Intriguingly Copping's oeuvre also includes illustrations for an 1895 girls' novel, *Willful Joyce*, whose titular character is described in a contemporary review as being, despite her willfulness, "a thoroughly healthy young creature whose mischievous escapades form very interesting reading" (*The Publisher's Circular*, Christmas 1895, 13).

Whether or not Harold Copping's surviving daughter Joyce, aka Elizabeth, was herself "willful," her choice of marriage partners certainly was out of the common rut. Both of her husbands were extremely talented men with an affinity for art. In 1921, when she was only 19, Elizabeth wed Kenneth de Burgh Codrington (1899-1986), a brilliant young colonial Englishman then studying Indian archaeology at Oxford. (Like Agatha Christie, Elizabeth made a marital match with an archaeologist, though, to be sure, it was a union of much shorter duration.) Less than six years later the couple were divorced, with Elizabeth seeming to express ambivalent feelings about her first husband in her second detective novel, *What Dread Hand?* After his divorce from Elizabeth, Codrington, who corresponded about matters of religious philosophy with T.S. Eliot, would become Keeper of the Indian Museum at the Victoria and Albert Museum, London, and later the first professor of Indian archaeology at London's School of Oriental and African Studies. Codrington's "affection and respect for Indian culture," notes an authority on colonial Indian history, "led him to a strong belief in a mid-century ideal of universal humanity" (Saloni Mathur, *India by Design: Colonial History and Cultural Display*)—though presumably this was not to be under the specifically Christian banner metaphorically unfurled in Harold Copping's "The Hope of the World."

In 1927 Elizabeth wed a second time, this time to Colin Unwin Gill (1892-1940), a prominent English painter and muralist and cousin of the controversial British sculptor Eric Gill. As was the case with his new bride, Colin Gill's first marriage had ended in divorce. A veteran of the Great War, where he served in the Royal Engineers as a front-line camouflage officer, Colin was invalided back to England with gas poisoning in 1918. In much of his best-known work, including *Heavy Artillery* (1919), he drew directly from his own combat experience in France, although in the year of his marriage to Elizabeth he completed one of his finest pieces, inspired by English medieval history, *King Alfred's Longships Defeat the Danes, 877*, which was unveiled with fanfare at St. Stephen's Hall in the Palace of Westminster, the meeting place of the British Parliament, by Prime Minister Stanley Baldwin.

During the seven years of Elizabeth and Colin's marriage, which ended in 1934 with Elizabeth's premature death, the couple resided at a ground-floor studio flat at the Tower House, Tite Street, Chelsea--the same one, indeed, where James McNeill Whistler, the famous painter and a great-uncle of the mystery writer Molly Thynne, had also once lived and worked. (Other notable one-time residents of Tite Street include writers Oscar Wilde and Radclyffe Hall, composer Peter Warlock, and artists John Singer Sargent, Augustus John and Hannah Gluckstein, aka "Gluck"—see Devon Cox's recently collective biography of famous Tite Street denizens, *The Street of Wonderful Possibilities: Whistler, Wilde and Sargent in Tite Street*.) Designed by progressive architect William Edward Godwin, a leading light in the Aesthetic Movement, the picturesque Tower House was, as described in *The British Architect* ("Rambles in London Streets: Chelsea District," 3 December 1892, p. 403), "divided into four great stories of studios," each of them with a "corresponding set of chambers formed by the introduction of a mezzanine floor, at about half the height of the studio." Given the strongly-conveyed settings of Elizabeth's first two detective novels, the first of which she began writing not long after her marriage to Colin, I surmise that the couple also spent a great deal of their time in southern France.

Despite Elizabeth Gill's successful embarkation upon a career as a detective novelist (she also dabbled in watercolors, like her great-grandfather, as well as dress design), dark clouds loomed forebodingly on her horizon. In the early 1930s her husband commenced a sexual affair with another tenant at the Tower House: Mabel Lethbridge (1900-1968), then the youngest recipient of the Order of the British Empire (O.B.E.), which had been awarded to her for her services as a munitions worker in the Great War. As a teenager Lethbridge had lost her left leg when a shell she was packing exploded, an event recounted by her in her bestselling autobiography, *Fortune Grass*. The book was published several months after Elizabeth's death, which occurred suddenly and unexpectedly after the mystery writer underwent an operation in a West London hospital in June 1934. Elizabeth was laid to rest in Shoreham, Kent, beside her parents, who had barely predeceased her. In 1938 Colin married again, though his new wife was not Mabel Lethbridge, but rather South African journalist Una Elizabeth Kellett Long (1909-1984), with whom Colin, under the joint pseudonym Richard Saxby, co-authored a crime thriller, *Five Came to London* (1938). Colin would himself pass away in 1940, just six years after Elizabeth, expiring from illness in South Africa, where he had traveled with Una to paint murals at the Johannesburg Magistrates' Courts.

While Kenneth de Burgh Codrington continues to receive his due in studies of Indian antiquities and Colin Gill maintains a foothold in the annals of British art history, Elizabeth Gill's place in Golden Age British detective fiction was for decades largely forgotten. Happily this long period of unmerited neglect has ended with the reprinting by Dean Street Press of Elizabeth Gill's fine trio of Benvenuto Brown mysteries. The American poet, critic, editor and journalist Amy Bonner aptly appraised Elizabeth's talent as a detective novelist in her *Brooklyn Eagle* review of the final Gill mystery novel, *Crime De Luxe*, writing glowingly that "Miss Gill is a consummate artist. . . . she writes detective stories like a novelist. . . . [Her work] may be unhesitatingly recommended to detective fiction fans and others who want to be converted."

CRIME DE LUXE

Why, indeed, he thought peevishly, couldn't people murder each other on dry land instead of intruding upon this pleasant and highly artificial board-ship life their personal feuds? It seemed to him at the moment like a breach of manners.

IN *CRIME DE LUXE*, Elizabeth Gill's final Benevenuto Brown detective novel, the author eschews the southern France settings of her two previous mysteries, in favor of a transatlantic luxury ocean liner, the mythically-named Atalanta, on which the artist and amateur detective is traveling to New York, where a gallery is to hold an exhibition of his paintings. Among the passengers Brown meets on board Atalanta during his five days ocean crossing are the quaintly English Mr. and Mrs. Pindlebury, she seeming to Brown on first impression rather a dear . . . though a foolish dear" and he something rather like a "Surtees squire" (this a reference to R.S. Surtees, master of Hamsterley Hall in County Durham and a Victorian era author of such novels as Handley Cross, Hillingdon Hall and Hawbuck Grange, many of which were illustrated by the great Punch caricaturist John Leech); the nouveau riche Lord Stoke, the latest vulgar "ornament to the British peerage," and Lady Stoke, "his Follies-girl wife"; the effortlessly alluring young widow Ann Stewart, who emphatically catches Brown's charmed eye; Mr. Leonard Growling, whom Brown mentally labels "the bicycle agent"; Mr. Morton-Blount, avowed Communist and a fervent admirer of the Soviet experiment; the enigmatic and oddly out-of-date Miss Smith, who brings to Brown's mind the lyrics of the popular Victorian song "Daisy Bell (Bicycle Built for Two)" (Daisy, Daisy, I'm just crazy/All for the love of you); gorgeous Rutland King, "the greatest lover on the screen"; and an elusive American blonde. Benevenuto Brown quickly discovers that there are dangerous undercurrents eddying about these passengers; and, soon enough, he finds himself assisting yet another murder investigation, his fame as an amateur sleuth having preceded him on board. This time around Inspector Leech, Brown's policeman friend in Gill's first two detective novels, is not present (though he does send the painter a clue clinching telegram), his place providentially being taken by "Ex-Inspector Markham, late of the C.I.D., New Scotland Yard."

Gill's skeptical portrayal of Lord Stoke and Mr. Morton-Blount, representatives of antipodal ideological poles (unrestrained capitalism and unfiltered Communism respectively), may well have been informed by circumstances in the author's own life. The family textile manufacturing firm of Gill's maternal great-grandfather and grandfather, both named James Mothersill, was liquidated in the 1880s, prompting the younger James Mothersill to relocate with his wife and eight children, including Elizabeth's mother, from Manchester to Islington, London, where he sold camera equipment for a living—rather a comedown for the family economically, which may have given Gill a sense of distaste for the vagaries of the marketplace and the predations of its more rapacious representatives. On the other hand, Gill in *Crime De Luxe* also adopts a skeptical stance toward alleged social advances being made at the time in the Soviet Union, despite the fact that her father's brother, journalist and author Arthur E. Copping, had gradually become, during his stint as Russian correspondent for the *London Daily Chronicle* in the years following the Great War, sympathetic to the Soviet cause, producing a series of nationally circulated pro-Bolshevik press articles about the U.S.S.R. that one anti-Bolshevik source sourly characterized as "insipid effusions." (See, for example, "INTO SOVIET RUSSIA WITH A GAY PARTY OF LENIN'S AGENTS: Correspondent Accompanies Them to Petrograd and Moscow to See for Himself" and

"MOSCOW ORDERLY UNDER RED RULE: Investigator Finds Bolsheviki Good Administrators and Enjoying Popular Support.") In contrast, Ann Stewart—something, one suspects, of an author mouthpiece, like, in the earlier novels, Julia Dallas and Adelaide Moon—speaks doubtfully concerning Mr. Morton Blount's millennialist idealization of the U.S.S.R.: "Roger has a religion, you see, though it's a social one. He believes Russia is the Promised Land. I don't know enough about it to know if he'd still think so if he went there. I expect so. He always sees what he expects to see."

At the midway point of the voyage (and the novel), an interesting discussion takes place among Ann Stewart, Benvenuto Brown and the Pindleburys, husband and wife, concerning the modern world and the modern woman, with Mr. Pindlebury giving voice to traditional British conservatism and Ann, in particular, taking a more iconoclastic, radically individualist view:

> Mr. Pindlebury shook his head vigorously. "Nonsense, sir. 'Tisn't growth, it's rot we're suffering from. I tell you, human beings knew what they were about when they fell into separate classes and invented the conventions. You can't play a game without abiding by the rules. When people start to cheat, it's the beginning of the end. Look at America—a country with even less respect for law and order and the conventions than we have ourselves. What's the result? Chaos, sir; bootleggers, gangsters, and kidnappers. Respectable citizens being shot down in the street. Battle, murder, and sudden death. Call that progress?
>
> "Yes," said Ann. "It's a sign of progress, or of vitality, at least. I can't see much difference between the gangsters of America and the men who went out and conquered half the world for England, except that they work on a smaller scale. We've got in the habit of calling them heroes and empire builders, but they were

mostly pirates and brigands, really. The point is that they all have the same quality—Francis Drake or Al Capone: the quality of personal courage. They are real people who go for what they want without counting the cost. That's why they're dangerous. . . . Don't you realize the old laws are no good? People have outgrown them, they're cunning, they can outwit them. Until we've built up some new ones to fit our new world, we have to act alone, on our own responsibility, according to our own lights—unless we want to sit back and be ruled by people who are dead and buried."

At the end of the voyage (and the novel), Benvenuto Brown, having solved his latest murder case, raptly gazes out from Atalanta's deck at the slowly materializing outline of New York City, thinking: "What a city to paint—what a city! El Greco would have liked it, he thought. Fra Angelico would have liked it—he'd have used it in a background for the Holy Family." Elizabeth Gill herself travelled by liner from the UK to the US several times, the first time in 1928 with her husband, Colin Gill, when Colin was serving on the award jury for the Carnegie International, the annual exhibition of contemporary art held at the Carnegie Museum of Art in Pittsburgh. Judging by *Crime de Luxe*, Elizabeth liked what she saw in America. Americans reading *Crime De Luxe* returned the favor, judging by contemporary notices. In the *Brooklyn Eagle* poet and critic Amy Booker praised Gill as a "novelist playing with intellectual ideas, like time; introducing Russian communism; describing and dressing her characters with the eye of a novelist; and giving the reader an altogether delightful treat"; while in the *New York Times Book Review* the novel received an unqualified rave from crime fiction critic Isaac Anderson, who with mock outrage complained:

Somebody has been holding out on us; otherwise we should have had an opportunity before this of meeting Benvenuto Brown, the painter detective, for there have been two other books about him. Those two books may have skipped by us in the days when publishers were putting out detective stories faster than they could possibly be reviewed. If so, it was just too bad, for Brown is distinctly worth meeting. . . . The story, besides being sufficiently baffling, is very well written and introduces a group of unusually well-drawn characters.

In the UK *Crime de Luxe* was published with a jacket design based on *The Arrival* (c. 1913), a Futurist painting by C.R.W. Nevinson, who was, like Colin Gill, one of the noteworthy English Great War artists. A contemporary article on *The Arrival* stated of the painting that "it resembles a Channel steamer after a violent collision with a pier. You detect funnels, smoke, gangplanks, distant hotels, numbers, posters all thrown into the melting-pot, so to speak." The dynamism and energy that is manifest in *The Arrival* powerfully conveys the modernist sentiments expressed in *Crime De Luxe*. The novel is a fitting final stroke from Elizabeth Gill, a writer most proficient in the fine art of murder who left this world far too soon.

Curtis Evans

THE FIRST DAY

CHAPTER I
TRANSATLANTIC

THE OCEAN LINER *Atalanta* was ready to make her hundredth voyage to New York.

For the hundredth time she had spent four days in Southampton Docks, four days during which men had swarmed over her like ants. Long before the last of the passengers had stepped off the gangway the stevedores had got at her, unloading mail sacks, luggage, motor cars, hundreds of tons of cargo; grimy muscular men who hurried up the gangways, into her sides, lifted, pushed, heaved at the load of treasure. Then, as soon as they'd stripped her, they started loading her again—four hundred more tons of cargo they'd given her; twenty thousand gallons of water; four thousand tons of oil.

Down in the engine rooms the engineers worked, overhauling, repairing, greasing; up in the cabins stewards cleaned and stripped and polished, threw away flowers, powder boxes, cigar-ends, magazines, erasing every trace of the personalities that, for a few days, had turned each cabin into something individual, alive, different from its fellow. Soon they were clean and bare, hung with fresh linen, waiting, cool and silent, to be reanimated by fresh travellers and their possessions.

Up on the decks seamen rubbed and scrubbed until the brass shone and the woodwork was white, while all the time into the sides of the ship poured a never-ending stream of merchandize, food, and drink. Fish, meat, potatoes, milk, game, caviar, a ton of ice-cream—it was like stocking up a luxury Ark ready for a Metro-Goldwyn Flood.

Now it was finished. Clean and replete, with the sunlight gleaming on her vast sides, powerful, magnificent, and a trifle bored, the *Atalanta* awaited her passengers.

Meanwhile the Ocean Liner Express was rushing through Hampshire towards the sea at sixty miles an hour. The train was crowded, mostly with homing Americans, for being early autumn it was the season when many of them return to their own country after a summer in Europe. They gave the English train a faintly unfamiliar air, an air of careless expensiveness and careful comfort. Also, unlike the English, they were able to converse in trains, and the clear-cut decisive and rather beautiful American voices contrasted oddly with the soft English countryside through which the train was passing. Or so thought an Englishman who made his way slowly down the corridor.

Decisive, that's it, he thought. They're a decisive people. They're not hesitating, fumbling, introspective, doubtful people like we are. And what a relief it is—how good it will be to get to a country where black and white are distinct instead of being part of a complicated and mysterious grey. To know what one likes and to go for it, that's the thing. I only hope, his thoughts ran on, that they'll decide to go for my paintings—for he was on his way to New York to be present at his first exhibition in America.

The decisiveness of Americans shows even in their clothes, he thought. When they travel they *look* like travellers. They have special coats made of camel hair, soft caps, rugs. Now I don't believe I look in the least like a traveller, he went on resentfully glancing at himself in a mirror as he turned into his compartment, and making a vague attempt to straighten his untidy fair hair. And indeed he looked very unlike his own conception of a decisive traveller, his possessions consisting of one large suitcase marked 'Wanted on Voyage,' a Burberry, a rather tattered volume of "Candide," a brown felt hat, and the flannel suit he wore which, though well cut, was far from new. He was about thirty-five, with a sunburnt face, a rather long nose, a rather long upper lip, and a good deal of humour in his mouth and his half closed blue eyes, and his name was Benvenuto Brown.

He sat down in his corner and looked out of the window at a swift-moving picture of a farmhouse, some children on a gate, meadows and streams, and ducks splashing in a pond. It was very beautiful in the morning sunlight, very English— but he didn't mind how fast the train hurtled onwards. Benvenuto Brown, painter, and confirmed traveller, who had lived an adventurous life in many lands, and had served in the British Intelligence during the war, was passionately excited at the prospect of his first visit to America.

His hand went to his breast pocket, and as he pulled out his cigarette case he looked across at the two people who shared his compartment. They were an elderly couple, obviously English; she fat and placid with vague blue eyes— rather a dear, thought Benvenuto, though a foolish dear; he, small and wiry and sharp-featured with a keen, intelligent face and a distinct air of the hunting-field—he reminded one of a Surtees squire.

"Do you mind," said Benvenuto, "if I smoke?"

She looked up vaguely from her knitting and smiled gently at him. "You know quite well," she said reprovingly, "that Pindlebury has been covering me with smoke for thirty years."

Her husband dropped the copy of *The Times* he was reading and turned sharply towards her. "Really, Margaret, really," he expostulated. "You don't know this young man from Adam. How can he be expected to be familiar with my habits for the last thirty years? And don't talk as though you were a side of bacon. Gross exaggeration. My apologies, sir," he went on, turning to Benvenuto, "you must excuse my wife. Absence of mind. Well intentioned. Try a cigar."

Mrs. Pindlebury dropped her knitting into her lap.

"Dear, dear, what *have* I said?" she murmured. "I *quite* thought you were a friend of ours—an *old* friend. So confusing. So many strangers on the train—and then, seeing you, you looked so much as though you *ought* to be. A friend, I mean."

"How perfectly charming of you," said Benvenuto, retrieving a ball of pink wool which had rolled beneath the seat, and handing it to her. "It's so precisely what one would wish to look like, isn't it? Somebody's friend."

Mrs. Pindlebury, reassured, returned to her knitting while throwing many nods and smiles at Benvenuto.

"Your first trip?" barked Mr. Pindlebury suddenly.

Benvenuto nodded over the cigar he was lighting.

"Staying long?" went on his questioner.

"To tell you the truth, I've no idea. I'm hoping to get some portraits to paint, so it may be anything from six months to six years."

Mr. Pindlebury grunted. "Take a good look at *that*, young man," he said, stabbing the landscape with his cigar, "you'll see nothing to touch it."

"You don't like America, sir?" inquired Benvenuto.

Mr. Pindlebury changed his position and grunted again.

"Not a question of like or dislike," he retorted. "Point is, 'tisn't English. Everything too big. Landscape too big. Coverts too big. Buildings, vegetable marrows, oysters—far too big. No sense in it. Try Blue Points, though."

"Blue Points?" inquired Benvenuto.

"Oysters. Quite good. Then there's soft-shelled crab. Baked with a dash of—Hullo, hullo! here we are. Come along, Margaret, hurry up. My card, sir. See you on the boat, I hope. There you go, dropping stitches—"

His last remark was addressed to his wife, who appeared to be getting somewhat involved with her pink wool. Benvenuto glanced at the card he held in his hand—

Mr. Samuel Pindlebury
Thurston Manor
Leicester.

—and slipped it into his pocket, hoping to make their further acquaintance.

The train was pulling into Southampton Docks and he leaned out of the window, tasting the first breath of salt air and enjoying the stir of excitement which he always felt on arriving at a sea-port. He could see the towering sides of great liners, impassive giants lying imprisoned in their docks, the sunlight touching their painted funnels to bright patches of colour. With a kind of friendly awe he read the famous names written on their bows, feeling as though he were meeting celebrities for the first time.

There in the Cunard dock was the black painted side of the *Berengaria* with her red funnels. Over there under the White Star flag lay the *Olympic*, and beyond—his cigar dropped from his fingers—was his own boat, the *Atalanta*, superb in her white magnificence. People could say what they liked—there was as much romance in these ocean monsters as there had ever been in the old four-masters. Their smooth sides rearing up in the sun filled him with a curious excitement, and he saw each one as a floating world, a supreme triumph of the pigmies whose creation it was, a gesture of defiance by civilization to the forces of darkness and storm and ice. Yes, they've brought it off all right, he thought. One's as safe inside the belly of a liner in mid-Atlantic as one is in Piccadilly Circus—probably a good deal safer.

Then he hailed a porter, bumped his head on the window, and was amused at himself for feeling as emotional as though he'd never been in a ship before, instead of having sailed half the seas of the world. There was something about these Transatlantic liners—

He relinquished his porter to the Pindleburys, and having said good-bye, jumped out in search of another. He found one and strolled down the platform towards the entrance to the quay, deciding that the *Atalanta* must be going to carry a full load if the first-class passengers were fair evidence. The platform was crowded with a slow-moving throng of expensive-looking people; whiffs of perfume and cigar smoke assailed his nose as he picked his way round piles of luggage and followed his porter towards a sign which read 'S.S. *Atalanta*, 1st class.' Dodging a group of smartly dressed women, some American children shepherded by their nurse, and a heap of cabin trunks and golf clubs, he ran down the steps.

Here was the *Atalanta* towering before him, clean, imposing, and larger than life-size. He sighed with satisfaction as he looked at her, welcoming the suave atmosphere of opulent peace which she seemed to promise him. He congratulated himself on having, somewhat optimistically, decided to travel first class. After a summer of really hard work in London, nothing could be pleasanter than five days of expensive sea breezes. He would devote himself whole-heartedly to the comforts of life, he thought, and do nothing more energetic than eat, sleep, stride round the deck and read the latest magazines. For five days no one could ring him up on the telephone—not even the post could disturb his impersonal existence. He wouldn't speak to a soul but his steward, except perhaps to pass the time of day with the Pindleburys. What bliss!

His pace becoming slower as the crowd approached the gangway, he looked about him at the fellow passengers he had decided to ignore. In the light of his new-found resolve they appeared as conventionally impersonal as he could wish, each one an archetype of the well-dressed ocean traveller. And how well-dressed they were, the men in English tweeds and travelling coats, the women soignée and beautifully tailored with just enough of a 'period' flavour subtly suggested in their clothes to make them elegantly feminine. The current fashions were charming, he decided. Immediately in front of him was a woman dressed in black, preparing to mount the first step of the gangway. Benvenuto Brown blinked and looked at her back view again. Something had gone wrong here. The costume in front of him was no creation of a modern couturier toying capriciously with the outlines of a vanished age. No. It was the genuine article. The stiff black cloth of the coat was seamed determinedly into the waist and flared out in the form of a basque—the shoulders were padded high, with sleeves that gathered stiffly into the armholes. In a flash Benvenuto was back in his school-days with a vision of his mother in just such a coat seeing him off at the station; and as he stared and wondered there floated down the breeze, like a tangible link with the past, the faint unmistakable odour of moth balls.

The next moment he was down on his knees collecting the scattered articles that strewed the quay, for the woman in front of him, in attempting to mount the gangway had let slip her black leather handbag which sent its contents flying. From between the feet of irritated travellers Benvenuto retrieved a leather purse, some keys, a handkerchief, a passport and the fragments of a bottle of smelling salts.

"I'm afraid this is done for," he said, smiling as he handed her bag and the broken bottle back to her. A pale lined face with thin lips and hollow dark eyes looked unsmilingly into his own.

"It is of no consequence. You are very good. I thank you, sir," said a nervously shaking voice, and she hurried up the gangway to the ship's side, clutching her bag beneath her antiquated sleeve.

Benvenuto Brown followed, mopping the fumes of smelling salts from his eyes. Here was an ocean traveller who did not conform to type.

CHAPTER II
WHO'S WHO?

"VISITORS OFF the ship, please!"

The voices of the stewards echoed through the entrance hall that resembled the foyer of a big hotel, and brought expressions of hastily concealed relief to the faces both of travellers and those who were performing the self-imposed and embarrassing duty of seeing them off.

Benvenuto Brown paused at the foot of the main staircase and congratulated himself on his success in discouraging all offers to accompany him down to the ship. What a distressing—what a positively dangerous custom this is of seeing people off, he decided, watching the sudden animation of final handshakes. It all begins so heartily. "What, sailing on Saturday?" one's friends say, "we'll run down and see you off," and foolishly, feeling rather grateful and flattered, one agrees.

Inevitably it is a failure. Louder than the rattle of the train is the sound of Time's winged chariot hurrying faster and faster, an accompaniment that makes one's lightest word fraught with significance, this being the last time we shall talk for—how long? Months, years perhaps. So we must be intelligent, tender, witty and of course cheerful. And gradually our expressions become fixed, our eyes glazed, our conversation jerky and our laughter unnaturally loud, so that by the time we have listened to the supreme inanity of our last-minute remarks we regard the former objects of our friendship or affection with positive loathing, and the signal for departure comes as a heaven-sent release. Happy is the friendless traveller, thought Benvenuto Brown, and stepping into the lift he was whirled up to C. deck.

He had secured an outside cabin, and having found it, he examined appreciatively its neat and luxurious efficiency. Indeed it was almost too luxurious—almost too much like an ordinary comfortable bedroom, with its gilt bedstead, its wardrobe, writing-table, easy chairs, and nothing but a porthole to remind one that one was a passenger on an ocean liner. He unlocked his suit-case and began to clean up for lunch.

Later, straightening his tie at the mirror, he paused, listening. A tremor, faint and delicious, had passed through the *Atalanta*; a tremor which wavered, steadied and changed to a quiet regular pulsation as though the hand of some life-giving deity had touched her, started her heart beating and sent the blood coursing through her veins. She had begun her voyage.

In the best of spirits Benvenuto left his cabin, and, hearing the summons of the lunch bugle, made his way to the dining-room.

The *maître d'hôtel* hurried forward, his fat pale face creased into a smile that seemed an anticipation of favours to come, and was perhaps half spontaneous at sight of this good-humoured-looking solitary passenger.

"Good morning, sir. Your cabin number, if you please. Ah yes, this way, Mr. Brown."

Benvenuto followed him through a forest of gleaming cutlery and linen to a single table against the wall, placed, he noticed with satisfaction, at a considerable distance from the band, and sat down in a chair held ready by a dinner steward. The menu was almost distressingly large and varied, but after a few moments' search his lunch took shape.

"Caviar, eggs Mornay, cutlets and peas," he said, refused a cocktail, ordered a pint of Pouilly, and sat back to examine his surroundings.

The brush of a contemporary painter had turned the walls into the semblance of a tropical jungle, and the band was playing a dance tune of African inspiration which contrasted oddly with the whiff of keen salt air that blew in through the open portholes. Benvenuto thought plaintively of the brass and white paint of more primitive vessels, and then gave himself up to studying his fellow passengers.

The dining-saloon was filling. From his seat against the wall he could see the big entrance doors and watch the progress down the room of the various groups of people. The *maître d'hôtel* darted here and there, busy and purposeful, sorting out his charges, piloting them to their particular tables, like a general disposing his men in some pre-ordained strategic plan. Freed from their outer coverings of travelling clothes and sorted into family groups, the passengers now appeared to Benvenuto as distinct personalities, each one an absorbingly interesting unit, a source of infinite speculation.

He took a draught of Pouilly, piled some excellent caviar on to hot toast, and sighed contentedly. For five days, alone, silent, and idle, he could, to his heart's content, play at his favourite game—a game he had played in the cafés of Paris, Vienna, Berlin and the sea-ports of the South—sitting back and watching the most superb entertainment in the world. People—unknown people, passing before him, the unconscious victims of his painter's eye and his restless imagination.

To Benvenuto it was the perfect recreation, the perfect antidote to his life of creative work and his occasional intense activity in criminal investigation. Where another sought refreshment or forgetfulness in the theatre, the cinema, or the latest novel, Benvenuto would go into a café and order a drink, and at once the entertainment would begin; an entertainment in which he reserved for himself the delight of creating the plot; weaving out of a dress, a gesture or a voice the story of a life, or finding in a face, a group, or an attitude, the stimulus for a painting.

He munched his caviar contentedly. This ship should mean five days' entertainment to him, he decided. He didn't know a soul on board. Except, of course, the Pindleburys. And thinking of them, he saw them sitting at a table some distance away, Mr. Pindlebury and the head waiter in solemn conference over the menu, while Mrs. Pindlebury bore an appearance of contented resignation, as of one who, though she is not consulted, realizes that all is for the best.

Then Benvenuto's view was obscured by a group passing by his table; a middle-aged couple, heavy with expensive fat and expensive clothes, while behind them, like a tiny yacht following two great barges, drifted an exquisite creature who was presumably, by some miracle of nature, their daughter. Her lovely face, and eyes that were two grey pools, turned towards Benvenuto and seemed occupied in absorbed contemplation of his person; then, as she raised a shell-white hand to her cropped hair, he realized there was a mirror behind his head. But the group had paused; the grey eyes flickered into consciousness of his existence, into an exciting approval of his existence, before they passed on. Slightly shaken, Benvenuto returned to his lunch. Possibly this business of being a Detached Observer shouldn't be taken too far.

By the time his eggs Mornay appeared the dining-saloon was almost full. On his left was an American family, father, mother and two sons, cultured, prosperous and good-looking; they were, perhaps, a University professor and his family, thought Benvenuto, Scotch blood mixed with good American stock. He was in the middle of apportioning to them a white pillared Colonial house and a Packard, when his attention was arrested by three people who had paused a few feet away, and were looking uncertainly about. Benvenuto dropped his fork and regarded them with delighted interest.

His own countrymen; but what bizarre train of events could have brought them together? There were two men and a woman, and it was to the smaller of the two men that Benvenuto's attention was first directed. His pale and watery eye, his drooping moustache and the tobacco-stained fingers that he passed nervously over it, his ill-fitting suit, butterfly collar, horse-shoe tie-pin, and tie whose stripes cried aloud to all regiments and all schools—these alone singled him out amongst the sleek and opulent travellers. He was a stage grocer—an undertaker's assistant—or, no—Benvenuto's fancy raced—he was a bicycle agent. And why in heaven's name was he travelling with these other two—this tall young man in horn-rimmed glasses whose loose limbs were clad in flannel trousers, and an old but perfectly cut tweed coat, whose limp dark hair hung in an untidy lock over his pale earnestly intellectual face, whose arm held a bundle of books and papers?

These two one might connect by means of a Social Welfare Tour, or an Education Conference—yet one glance at their companion sent his theories flying.

She was very tall and slender, and he noticed first her movements as she walked down the room. She moved exquisitely between the crowded tables, with a sure and elegant grace which caught the eye and held it. She moved, thought Benvenuto swiftly, as though she strolled barefoot across a lawn. She spoke to a waiter and her voice drifted across to him, cool and clear, and pitched a tone lower than all the women's voices round him. Then as she came towards him he saw her full-face and controlled an absurd desire to get up and speak to her, move a chair aside, do something to stop her before she passed by.

Instead, he watched the three incongruous backs following the waiter down the room, he drank some wine and tried to analyse his disturbance. It wasn't a question of beauty, for the woman who had passed did not compare with half the American girls round him. It wasn't vitality, for her face was pale, almost expressionless, as he saw it. In her face, her whole body, he had seen a quality of distinction, grace, sensitiveness—what was it? It was not even that which had held him; it was that her curious elusive quality had been overlaid by something else—by a strain, a tensity which isolated her from everyone.

He ate some food impatiently. It was probably all imagination, the woman had been tired from her journey—or she was recovering from an illness—or—well, whatever it was he knew he would have to see her again. From where he sat her back was visible—a tweed-covered back, a bare head of waving pale gold hair, and her hand, holding a cigarette. A commonplace Englishwoman's back, thought Benvenuto—and yet, confound her, there was an intangible glamour in the very way she smoked. She was speaking—speaking to the bicycle agent. Benvenuto threw down his napkin in unreasonable irritation and walked out on to the deck.

There was a storm cloud over England, but the *Atalanta*, gliding down Southampton Water towards the Solent, moved through brilliant sunlight. Benvenuto, stretched in a deck chair, watched the play of light and shade on ships and water against the dark background of cloud, saw the sun touch the white sails of a yacht, then the lavender and scarlet of an oil-driven liner, while flying shadows painted the water in patches of green and blue. They were leaving the clouds behind—ahead there were long days of sun and salt breezes.

He lit a cigarette and recovered his mood of amiable indolence, then jumped to his feet as Mr. and Mrs. Pindlebury, loaded with travelling rugs, magazines and knitting, paused in front of his chair.

"Tolerable lunch," remarked Mr. Pindlebury. "Hope they gave you something fit to eat. Let me know if they don't—I'll speak to the cook. Good man, but bone lazy. They all are."

"Thanks very much," said Benvenuto. "I certainly will. As a matter of fact I did very well." He took some books from Mrs. Pindlebury's hands. "Where are you going to sit?"

"Mind if we sit here?" Mr. Pindlebury summoned a steward who was hovering in the background with two deck chairs, and in a moment they were both comfortably installed, Mr. Pindlebury being rolled tightly in a rug from which his head emerged like that of a well-preserved mummy, while his wife seemed inextricably entangled in a whirl of pink wool and knitting needles from which she continually looked up to smile and nod at Benvenuto, as though in some secret understanding with him.

Mr. Pindlebury sniffed the breeze like an ancient pointer. "Good weather ahead," he remarked. "Not that I mind—don't suffer from sea-sickness. In fact, a rough passage is all to the good. Sends the land lubbers down below and you get more attention from the kitchen."

"Have you travelled in this boat before?" inquired Benvenuto.

"My twenty-second trip," replied Mr. Pindlebury. "Captain's a friend of mine. Good fellow; you must meet him. By the way, are you Brown the painter who was mixed up in that business of young Kulligrew's death? Ah—thought you must be. I know Rourke and his wife, and I heard a lot about you from them. Smart piece of work, young man. Often thought I'd like to be a policeman. Trouble is, we're all liars and half of us are rogues. Difficult business, fixing the guilt on one when it might be any one of half a dozen. Take that case in the paper last week—"

In a moment they were deep in argument over the problems of the latest murder, and Benvenuto was only brought back to consciousness of his surroundings by the sight of the tall fair-haired Englishwoman walking past him in conversation with the bespectacled young man.

"That's an interesting-looking woman," he said abruptly.

Mr. Pindlebury sat up with a start and fumbled for his eye-glass. But his expression changed to one of disapproval at sight of the retreating figure. "Too thin," he muttered. "Far too thin. Hate to see a woman's bones. No comfort without curves. If they're bony, they should pad. My mother did. I remember as a boy seeing them on the dressing-table." He sketched two vague circles in the air with his hands. "Horsehair, I believe. Illusion perfect. Sensible woman."

"Now, now, Pindlebury," murmured his wife vaguely from behind her knitting needles.

"Nonsense, my dear, nonsense," retorted Mr. Pindlebury, as though in answer to some provocative statement. "Brown agrees with me. Sensible fellow."

But Benvenuto Brown, following with his eyes the elegant and well-tailored back of the unknown woman, kept his opinion to himself.

Suddenly as he watched her she paused, touched her companion's arm, and pointed across the water. In a few moments she was the centre of a group of people bending over the ship's rail, looking at some incident below. Benvenuto got to his feet and walked over to the side followed by the Pindleburys.

A steam tender was rapidly approaching the ship, the water creaming in its wake, the sunlight touching its white paint and shining metal. On its deck were a group of people, and as they drew nearer Benvenuto could distinguish a stout man and a slender and excessively smart girl, backed by a mountain of luggage and several nondescript figures in attendance. In a moment the launch had made fast to the ship's side; as he turned away Benvenuto came face to face with the tall Englishwoman and looked at her in surprise. She was no longer pale and expressionless; instead she seemed alight with suppressed excitement and was holding tightly to her companion's arm.

"Thank Heaven," he heard her say.

Really, he decided, she becomes more and more intriguing. Her friends now number a bicycle agent, an intellectual young man, and the new arrivals who are, apparently, profiteers. His thoughts were interrupted by Mr. Pindlebury who moved away from the ship's side unscrewing his monocle.

"That," he remarked, "was Lord Stoke, the newest ornament to the British peerage, and his Follies Girl wife. Why— God bless my soul—here's Ann!"

Mr. Pindlebury was beaming, and shaking the intriguing woman warmly by the hand.

CHAPTER III
MOTH BALLS

BRILLIANT with lights, loaded with rich foods and wines, perfumes, flowers, and silks, the *Atalanta* carried her cargo of passengers swiftly through the dark sea. Outside on the decks couples strolled, arm-in-arm, watching the stars and the oily swell of black water. Women's evening gowns gleamed palely against the darkness, and the scent of after-dinner cigars floated down the breeze. Inside, in the white and gold ballroom, other couples swayed to a Viennese waltz, and old women, sitting against the wall, nodded their heads in time to the music, thought of their lost youth, and prayed for a smooth passage. Down below in the service quarters the stewards had thrown off their coats and were playing cards, writing letters, and calculating the probable tipping capacity of their latest charges.

It was a compact, highly organized, highly civilized world, existing transitorily between dark water and dark sky.

In the smoking-room Mr. Pindlebury raised a glass of brandy to his lips, set it down, puffed at his excellent cigar, and sighed.

"It was a sad business," he said, turning in his chair towards Benvenuto Brown. "I've known Ann Garstin—Ann Stewart she now is—since the first day she sat in a saddle. A fine child, with fat legs, I remember. Lord! how they change! She created a storm the year she came out, half the men in London at her feet. She could have mated with the best stock in the country. Instead of which she married young Tom Stewart."

"You mean the biologist who was killed in a motor smash some months ago?"

Mr. Pindlebury nodded over his drink.

"I remember something about it," said Benvenuto, "but I was out of England at the time, working on a case. So it was her husband—"

"Yes. A bad business altogether. He was a brilliant man they tell me, and a great loss. Ann's a changed woman. Gave me a shock when I saw her to-day. Lost her spirit. Looks as if she could see ghosts. What made it all the harder for her was that some fool started a rumour that there'd been foul play—car tampered with. All nonsense, of course. People will say anything for a bit of drama." He got to his feet. "Suppose we join the women?"

Together they walked to the ballroom and stood for a moment watching the dancers. Mr. Pindlebury screwed in his eye-glass.

"Deplorable," he remarked. "I shall never get used to 'em. Why, they're like a lot of young lads. If only they'd realize—women, and Burgundy, should be full bodied. You ought to have seen them in *my* day—" a reminiscent gleam came into his eye. "They had a presence, a carriage—Queenly creatures, every one of 'em. A fine woman waltzing in a ballroom was a pretty sight—feathers—laces—a fan—low-cut bodice, and a flash of petticoats. Ah!" He sighed. "Very different matter from these flat-fronted snake-hipped harpies. There's nothing *there*—nothing to get hold of. Nothing to lead a man on."

"And yet," murmured Benvenuto, "surely that has something to recommend it."

In the doorway, dressed in a long slender white dress, her fair head rising from the fluttering white feathers of a tiny shoulder cape, stood the American blonde he had noticed at lunch time. Sleek, soignée, and perfumed, arrogantly young and exquisite, she stood for a moment indolently watching the dancers with enormous delicately painted eyes, and then strolled down the room. Mr. Pindlebury, screwing his eye-glass more firmly into position, automatically started to move after her, but Benvenuto laid a restraining hand on his arm.

"I think," he said, "that I can see Mrs. Pindlebury over there—and isn't that Mrs. Stewart with her?"

"Ah yes, so it is," said Mr. Pindlebury, with an air of frustration. Turning, they both walked towards a sofa where Mrs. Pindlebury and Ann Stewart were seated talking to two men. With rising interest Benvenuto saw that they were Mrs. Stewart's companions at table; in a moment he was being introduced to them.

"Mr. Leonard Gowling, Mr. Brown," said Mrs. Stewart.

"Pleased," said the bicycle agent, as he shook hands, "to meet you."

"And, Mr. Morton-Blount, Mr. Brown," she went on.

The tall young man peered short-sightedly at Benvenuto through his glasses, and greeting him, dropped a bundle of books and papers on to the floor. When he had collected them he placed them carefully on the sofa.

"Shall we dance?" he said to Ann. In a moment he was moving clumsily across the floor with her in his arms, and Benvenuto excused himself and strolled out on deck.

Now that he had met her, knew her name and her history, Ann Stewart remained as incomprehensible as before. With Mr. Pindlebury's story in his mind he tried to reconcile it with his impressions of her, tried to make a coherent whole. During the few moments when he had met and spoken to her, his sense of her strained detachment had been strengthened. She was not, he felt, a woman broken with grief. She was a woman obsessed by some particular thing, tense and purposeful. And thinking of her he felt that he must, somehow, break through her detachment.

He turned back towards the dance-room, then stopped at sight of a hesitant figure who had just risen from a deck chair and was looking about her. A white face stared at him in a frightened way, and as she moved towards him he smelt the depressing, musty odour of moth balls. It was the woman whose bag he had retrieved from the quay.

"Excuse me—do you know the time?" she asked him in her nervous, shaking voice.

Benvenuto pulled his watch from his pocket.

"It's just ten o'clock," he said, and helped her back into her chair, arranging a shawl over her knees. As he was leaving she spoke again.

"You must pardon me for asking you, but—could you tell me the name of the man you were speaking to just now? I fear you will think me bold, but I thought—I thought I remembered him."

"Now I wonder," said Benvenuto, "what man you mean. Was it perhaps Mr. Pindlebury—Samuel Pindlebury, the elderly man I was with?"

"Oh, no—" she answered, "not that gentleman. The other one—who was with the beautiful lady."

"The small man with the moustache? Yes—his name was—let me see, Gowling, I think. I had that moment been introduced to him."

"Gowling." Her voice, he thought, sounded as though it was familiar. "Gowling," she repeated. "I—I must have been mistaken. Thank you very much." She had sunk back in her chair and seemed as though she wished him to go.

"Not a bit," he said. "Good night." He was turning away when once more her voice recalled him.

"Is it likely—to be a long voyage?"

Benvenuto looked at her in astonishment, then sat down beside her.

"It takes five days," he said. "Is this your first trip?"

"I beg your pardon? Oh, yes—yes—I am not—" she laughed huskily, "not a great traveller. In fact"—she leant towards him with a sudden rush of confidence, "I have not moved from one place in many years—many years. I forget how many." She drew back again, as though sorry she had spoken, and pulled her cloak round her, half hiding her face.

"Well, now that you've made a move, I hope you'll enjoy the voyage," said Benvenuto. "Won't you have a drink? It's getting a bit chilly out here."

She looked at him, startled. "Oh—you are very kind—very good. I—do you think I might have a glass of—of port wine?"

"Why, of course." Benvenuto half rose from his chair, but she caught at his arm with bony fingers. "Must we go inside? It is so wonderfully open—so free—" she finished, gesturing out into the darkness.

"No need to move at all. Here, Steward! Bring me a glass of port and a *fine*."

He leant back in his chair and studied his companion's profile. She was sitting bolt upright staring in front of her, the light from an open door shining on her face. It was difficult to tell her age—she might have been anything between forty and sixty. Her black, frizzy hair, streaked with grey, was piled up squarely above her forehead in a style reminiscent of Queen Alexandra; her eyes were black and sunken, her face deathly pale, with the horrible pallor of a plant grown in darkness. In her black, antiquated clothes, she was a figure of darkness. She would have been sinister, he thought, but for the pitiful droop of her thin lips and her hesitant, shaking, faintly common voice. He felt an extreme pity for her as he watched her and saw her bony fingers nervously fidgeting with the fringe of her shawl. What grim and gloomy life had brought her to this desolate state?

"This is my first trip, too," he said. "I am looking forward immensely to seeing New York. I expect you are."

"New York?" She had turned, and was staring at him in a bewildered way, for all the world, he thought, as though she did not know where the ship was heading.

"New York," she repeated slowly. "I remember my sister Sally went there with her husband. They were emigrants."

"You will be pleased to see them," ventured Benvenuto. But she shook her head in a puzzled way. "I don't know—perhaps they have gone. I was never allowed to write. Why, do you think I could find them? But no—no—I mustn't do that—"

He bent forward to take her glass from a tray the steward handed to him, and gave it to her, then raised his own towards her before he drank. She looked at him, then down at the glass in her hand. Slowly, with a shaking hand, she raised it high in the air with a pitiful and gallant gesture, and drank as though to some long forgotten memory. Benvenuto was disturbed to see, as she put her glass down, a tear-drop glistening on her cheek.

"You are very kind, wonderfully kind." Then, abruptly: "How old are you?" she asked.

"I think I'm thirty-six," answered Benvenuto, smiling.

"Ah! You are older than my son."

"Is your son in America?" asked Benvenuto.

"Oh, no. He is in Heaven." Her voice was very calm and matter-of-fact, so that he wondered for a moment if he had heard aright. Then with a nervous movement, she half sprang from her chair. "Oh—what is the time—please tell me—"

He got up and looked at his watch. "It is nearly half-past ten," he said.

She gathered her shawl swiftly round her. "I must go—to my cabin. You have been so good and kind, you have made me forget. Good-bye." With a stiff little bow she was gone. He stood for a moment looking after the black figure as it hurried jerkily down the corridor. When she had disappeared, there still remained the musty, camphorated smell; no perfume, he thought, could have suited her better.

He went and leant over the ship's rail and sniffed the breeze. He could hear dance music above the sound of the water, and he turned and went into the ballroom.

CHAPTER IV
DARK WATERS

THE WHITE and gold ballroom was crowded with dancers. Benvenuto Brown stood for a moment at the door, then made his way towards a settee on which were sitting Mr. and Mrs. Pindlebury, and between them, Ann Stewart. As he approached he saw that they were getting up.

"Here you are," remarked Mr. Pindlebury. "My wife is going to bed. I'll see you later."

Mrs. Pindlebury held her hand out to Benvenuto. "A little tired," she said, nodding brightly. "Good night. Thank you *so* much," she added ambiguously, with a perfect battery of smiling nods. But he had no time to wonder what she meant; Ann Stewart was turning away with the other two. "I was coming," he said, "to ask you if you'd dance with me."

She looked at him gravely, and from a distance, it seemed to him, of several miles. He thought she was going to refuse, when suddenly Mrs. Pindlebury interposed. "Now, Ann, you must dance with Mr. Brown. He's *such* a good dancer. It is good for young people to amuse themselves. Why, I remember as a girl I often danced through my slippers. I have quite a collection of little programmes, all full. Such pretty pencils. Now dance, dear, and enjoy yourself."

Ann's face softened as she bent and kissed her. "Of course I am going to enjoy myself."

Benvenuto was fond of dancing, and as they moved on to the floor he knew that he had found a perfect partner.

"I am afraid," he said, "that Mrs. Pindlebury deceived you. She was hazarding a wild guess."

"You dance beautifully." Ann's delicious voice, cool and clear, was so utterly impersonal that he felt quite chilled. They danced for a little in silence, and then she spoke again.

"I always feel guilty," she said, "towards the old, unless I can live up to their standards of gaiety. Margaret Pindlebury is a darling. For her the world is a pleasant place, half flower garden and half drawing-room, where people are gentle with each other and kind to animals. When I am with her I have to pretend it is true."

"The great point about people like that," said Benvenuto, "is that they make it true. Their world is just as real as, say, yours or mine. And they are perpetually holding out to us a kind of spiritual umbrella under which we can shelter."

"The pathetic part of it is," said Ann, "that in a really bad storm the umbrella would simply get blown inside out."

"Quite so. I never use them myself," he said, and wondered how in the world he could make her smile, come to life. Even while she talked, one half of her was far away, brooding and aloof, occupied in some secret and passionate existence. She was silent now, and he found her silence less of a barrier than her cool, low-toned speech. When the dance ended she looked directly at him and smiled faintly. They had moved perfectly together.

"Will you come on deck?" said Benvenuto. "It's a pleasant night." She picked up her cloak and walked silently beside him. She appeared, he noted, with rueful approval, to have no use for small talk.

"I think I've seen your friend Morton-Blount before," he said, lying, in an attempt to draw her into something personal. "Is he a writer?"

"No," said Ann, "but he has a Mission. Roger's tragedy is that he was born just too late. He will never cease to regret that he wasn't in the war,—as a Conscientious-Objector. However, he still finds plenty of things to conscientiously object to. He's a charming and enviable character, you know. For him life *is* real and earnest. Everything matters to him; at least, everything impersonal."

"When you say he is enviable, you mean—things *don't* matter to you?"

"Not in Roger's way. Why, I can't imagine anything more perfect than to have a definite religion, for instance. Something you could really believe in. Roger has a religion, though it's a social one. He believes Russia is the Promised Land. I don't know enough about it to know if he'd still think so if he went there. I expect so. He always sees what he expects to see. You mustn't mind," for a moment her voice rippled with laughter, "if he calls you Brother. It always makes me want to cry when he does it, because he's so out of touch with life. All the same, I have always envied him."

"I suspect," said Benvenuto, "that there are plenty of things to recompense you for not having a Mission. For one thing, you will always be able to see things you don't expect to see, which is half the fun of life. I believe myself that every time you fix your eye on some future state of perfection, whether it's spiritual or temporal, you are probably missing something which is going on under your nose. And surely it takes the zest out of any adventure if you're sure of a safe harbour at the end of it."

Ann looked at him curiously. "You talk," she said, "as if being alive suited you very well. You are lucky."

She turned away, and leaning over the rail of the ship she looked down into the black water. With a clear, flute-like sound she began to whistle a tune, a curious, half-reckless, half-plaintive tune, that troubled his ear because he knew it and could not place it. The notes fell and rose, and he felt that if he walked away from her she would not notice his absence or ever think of him again.

Her last words echoed in his mind: "You are lucky." They had had about them an impersonal finality which made them sound like his epitaph, so far as she was concerned. He felt disturbed and badly thwarted, as though he had seen into some rarely beautiful country of great mountains and rich pastures, and at the frontier he had been barred from exploring it. She had talked to him with a cool carelessness that was in direct contradiction to his impression of her—an impression of tragic, high-strung recklessness. Would he ever reach her?

As her tune ended there was a sudden silence. Benvenuto emerged from his thoughts with a shock. What was wrong? It was an unnatural silence—an enormous, infinite silence, loud and significant as a thunderclap.

The ship's engines had stopped.

Ann turned and stared at him with startled eyes, then with one accord they hurried over to the other side where a confused shouting sounded from the decks below. In a moment Benvenuto was running down the companion-way, Ann at his heels. As they reached the deck a steward rushed past them. "Man overboard!" he said. By now, the ship was alive with bells ringing and hurrying feet, and the *Atalanta* appeared to be turning in a field of swirling waters. With incredible speed, boats were manned and lowered, and a great searchlight, turned on to the sea, isolated a path of water in a parody of daylight, ghastly and sharpened.

Beside him, pressing forward over the ship's rail, Ann Stewart was crushed by the crowd close against Benvenuto's side. He could feel her body shaken with trembling, and hear her breath coming fast through her parted lips. He looked along the line of faces peering over the side, at their varying expressions of curiosity, horror, excitement and fear, then at Ann's face, so close to his own. With growing amazement he watched her. Some emotion, very different from those which stirred the other watchers, was at work here; her eyes were blazing in her pale face, her lips twitching, and she was shaken, he could have sworn, by a mixture of surprise and—anger.

Did she know who it was, down there in the dark water? He felt a conviction that she did.

Now she had turned and was looking past him, oblivious of his presence, searching for someone. In the long moments of waiting which followed, he, too, looked about amongst the crowded faces. So far as he could see, neither Gowling nor

Morton-Blount were present; possibly they were watching from another deck.

Suddenly he heard a shout, and with the swift reaction of a waiting crowd all the people about him pressed forward. In the distance, sharply defined in the cold glaring light, the boats had reached a lighted buoy which had been flung overboard, and in one of them a seaman was standing, signalling with his arms.

Their quest was at an end.

It was impossible to see what had happened, and for what seemed an eternity the hundreds of watchers waited silently as the little boats pulled slowly back towards the ship. As they drew near, a faint, communal sound came from the crowd, for in the nearest boat they could see a man bending over something which lay there, dark and still. At last the boat reached the ship's side while the others waited, rocking gently on the water.

Immediately below him, lying limp in a seaman's arms, Benvenuto saw for a moment in the glaring light the white face and black soaked figure of the woman he had talked with on deck not an hour before.

Swiftly he looked round at Ann. She was staring at the limp figure, her hands gripping the rail, and as he watched, the momentary pity and horror in her face were replaced by something else—by relief, and, he could have sworn it, joy.

He turned, and quickly edged his way through the crowd. He ran up the companion-way, and pausing at the top, examined the people below. Morton-Blount and Gowling were not there. On the deck above he moved swiftly through the groups of people who were talking in hushed voices, but after five minutes' search he turned away. They were not there. His task was more difficult now, for all the people were dispersing, going indoors. Following a sudden impulse, he hurried in and made his way to the purser's office. Outside it was hanging the passenger list, and he ran his eye down the names. Gowling, Mr. Leonard, Cabin 27, D. Deck, he read. Then, further on, Morton-Blount, Mr. Roger. Cabin 26, D. Deck. He hurried into the lift. On D. deck the corridor was deserted, everyone having scattered to watch the rescue. He tapped on the door of No. 26, but there was no reply. The door was unlocked, and he walked in and switched on the light.

The cabin was neat and empty, the bed turned down for the night, but undisturbed. He went out and tried the cabin next door, to find it in the same state. Whatever Morton-Blount and Gowling were doing whilst he had danced and talked with Ann, they had not been preparing for bed.

He paused for a moment in the corridor, his thoughts racing. The events of the evening passed before him as a series of pictures, each one isolated yet each one bearing a seeming relation to the next, forming a pattern, signifying—what?

He saw the tragic pallid face of the black dressed woman, her fears, her hesitancy; saw her again as she peered at him, questioning him about Gowling. He saw Ann, staring into the darkness, whistling her curious tune, aloof and incomprehensible; Ann again, bending over the ship's rail with the watching crowd, her body shaking, her face with its strange expression of surprise and anger. Then the boat, clear cut in the bright light, the seaman with his limp pathetic burden; again Ann—and here his mind swerved trying to refuse his memory of her face, alight with relief, with something more—something that had seemed like joy.

He walked quickly down the corridor. The first thing he must do, even before he discovered if the woman were really dead, was to find Morton-Blount and Gowling. As he passed he looked into the dance-room; it was empty, the lights blazing, the musicians' instruments left in disorder. In the writing-room a solitary couple sat on a settee; the library was deserted. He hurried on to the big lounge which was crowded and humming with subdued conversation, but after a few moments' search he knew they were not there. On the deck below, he drew blank in the smoking-room, and then went into the bar. With a feeling of elation he saw that he had found his quarry, for over in the far corner at a secluded table Morton-Blount and Gowling were sitting, talking in low tones.

Benvenuto went to the bar and bought himself a drink, then strolled across the room with it in his hand and sat down with his back to their table. But his drink stood untasted while he listened to the conversation behind him.

The two men, with an impassioned, an almost religious fervour, were discussing artificial manure.

CHAPTER V
INTERROGATION

THERE WAS a pause. Then—

"What makes the Criminal?" demanded Morton-Blount fiercely of his companion.

"Well, I 'ardly know," replied Mr. Gowling.

"Hunger," announced the other. "It is hunger that makes prostitutes, thieves and murderers. In a world freed from the menace of hunger, crime and Capitalism would cease to exist. In agriculture, as we now understand it, lies the salvation of man. Fertilization—"

Morton-Blount's eloquence, which in his excitement had risen in tone as though he were addressing a meeting, came to a sudden end. Benvenuto, still clutching the untasted drink, felt a conviction, as sure as though he had witnessed the incident, that Gowling had raised a warning hand. Blount's speech, apart from a slight tendency to rhetoric, seemed to Benvenuto's listening ears to be entirely blameless; it was merely the outpouring of an earnest young man with an agricultural bee in his bonnet. Why then, the necessity for caution? The two men were exchanging remarks in so low a tone that Benvenuto missed them, and then there was the sound of chairs scraping back.

"Well, it's time I was in bed," said Gowling loudly.

They walked past him to the door without, apparently, recognizing him; Gowling slightly flushed as though from an unusual indulgence in alcohol, Morton-Blount with his head poked short-sightedly forward on his shoulders, and his lock of dark hair falling on to the rim of his spectacles. Beneath his arm was the inevitable bundle of books and papers.

"I shall take the opportunity of doing a little serious work," he was saying. "I find that the brain—"

The rest of his sentence was lost as they passed on, but Benvenuto could see Gowling nodding his head in sympathetic agreement. They were surely the strangest pair who ever travelled together.

Was it possible, wondered Benvenuto, that they had sat there engrossed in their discussion to the exclusion of everything else, and were ignorant of the tragedy which had taken place? He must talk to Gowling before he went to bed, he decided, and hurried out of the bar. At the end of the corridor he could see them both waiting for the lift; he would go up afterwards and follow Gowling to his cabin. As he watched, the brass gates opened and Morton-Blount stepped inside, but Gowling, to his surprise, did not accompany him. Instead, he said good-night and walked across to the door opening on to the deck. Excellent, thought Benvenuto, and went after him.

The deck was deserted, everyone having, apparently, lost their taste for the night air since the recent tragedy. Benvenuto stood still looking about him, and it was a moment before he saw, in the distance, a small figure sidling surreptitiously along in the shadow.

Benvenuto drew back into the shadow of a doorway.

The figure ahead paused, looked nervously round, then standing on tiptoe, he peered into the half-opened window of one of the cabins. The light fell for a moment on to his face before he hurried away out of sight, but Benvenuto had seen that the furtive watcher was Gowling.

He walked slowly after him, counting the number of windows as he passed. Reaching the window into which Gowling had looked, he turned back, reentered the corridor and went along to the door of the interesting cabin. It was, he realized, a private suite, and he bent to look at the name-card on the door. 'Lord and Lady Stoke.'

In a moment he remembered—the steam tender catching up the ship, and Mr. Pindlebury recognizing the people on board—"the newest ornament to the Peerage and his Follies Girl wife," he had said. Then Ann, excited at seeing them, murmuring "Thank Heaven!" to her companion as she saw the Stokes come aboard. Always Ann—every thread seemed to lead back to her. Rather wearily Benvenuto went along to his cabin; he wanted to be alone and to think.

He had taken off his dinner jacket and was filling his pipe for a quiet smoke, when there was a knock on the door.

"Come in," he said irritably.

A steward was standing in the doorway. "The Captain's compliments, sir, and he'd be obliged if you'd spare him a few moments."

Considerably startled, Benvenuto laid down his pipe, put on his coat and followed the steward down the corridor. Standing in the lift, he noticed the impassive face of his guide. He had a good memory for faces, and after a moment he realized that it was the steward who had served him with drinks on deck whilst he had sat with the woman who was now, presumably, dead. What fresh development was in the wind?

On leaving the lift, a few moments' walk brought them up near the bridge, and on to official territory. The steward tapped on a door, and Benvenuto found himself in a bare map-hung room which was apparently the Captain's office. There were two men in the room, one an undistinguished-looking person in civilian clothes who was standing beside a large mahogany desk, while the other who was seated at the desk, telephone in hand, was a handsome white-haired man of fifty or sixty, dressed in Commodore's uniform. Benvenuto recognized the square head, bronzed features and shaggy eye-brows; it was Sir George Beckworth, Commodore of the Atlantic Fleet, a fine sailor and a likeable looking man, he thought. He was speaking into the telephone.

"No hope, you think? H'm—well, do your best; and report developments to me."

He replaced the receiver, looked across at Benvenuto with shrewd blue eyes which had a penetrating quality beneath their overhanging brows, and rose to his feet.

"Mr. Brown? Will you sit there?" He motioned to a chair opposite him. "I am sorry to bring you from your cabin at this hour. This is Inspector Markham, who is investigating the tragic accident which occurred this evening. He would like to ask you a few questions and I shall be grateful if you will give him what information you can."

"Certainly, sir," replied Benvenuto.

Ex-Inspector Markham, late of the C.I.D., cleared his throat and looked at Benvenuto pugnaciously. He was a tough-looking individual with a blue chin. His voice, however, was unexpectedly mild.

"You are Mr. Benvenuto Brown, of Glebe Gardens, Cheyne Walk, London?" he asked.

"Yes."

"Your profession is—"

"I am a painter."

"A painter? Oh, yes, an artist. Thank you, Mr. Brown. What was the name of the lady you were sitting with on the promenade deck this evening?"

"I have no idea," replied Benvenuto, "if you mean the lady for whom I ordered a drink."

"I do. At what time did you part from her?"

"It was almost half-past ten."

The inspector looked at him suspiciously. "You are sure of the time?"

"Quite sure. She asked me the time once or twice, and left abruptly when I told her it was nearly ten-thirty."

"Ah! Did she mention where she was going?"

"She said she was going to her cabin. I gathered the impression that she had some definite objective other than going to bed, since she seemed anxious about the time."

"I see. How long have you known this lady?"

Benvenuto considered a moment. "Since ten o'clock this evening," he said.

The inspector looked at him again, then back to the notebook in which he was writing.

"When did you next see her?"

"I don't know the exact time, but when I next saw her, she was lying in the rescue boat. Can you tell me if she is likely to recover?"

The inspector turned to the Captain, who answered Benvenuto's question. "It is very doubtful," he said gravely.

"I'm sorry to hear that. Is there anything else I can tell you?"

"I shan't keep you much longer, Mr. Brown—" said the inspector. "Where were you between the time that Miss Smith left you and the time of the rescue?"

"I was in the ballroom, and afterwards on deck."

"Were you alone?"

"No. I was with a Mrs. Stewart." The inspector made another note in his book.

"Has this lady—Miss Smith—any relatives in America?" he said abruptly.

"I believe she has a married sister in New York."

"I see. Any children living?"

"She had a son who is dead. That is all I know."

"What was her address in England?"

"I have no idea."

"When was the last time you saw her in England?"

Benvenuto stared at him in surprise. "I have just told you, Inspector, I made the acquaintance of Miss Smith to-night at ten o'clock for the first time."

But the inspector was looking stonily at the Captain. There was silence for a moment; the Captain bent forward across the table and was about to speak when he was arrested by the buzzing of the telephone. He lifted the receiver.

"Yes. Yes, Doctor. Ah—I feared as much. Did she regain consciousness? I see. I will be down to the hospital in half an hour."

His face was grave as he addressed himself again to Benvenuto.

"Mr. Brown, I have no wish to intrude upon any personal matter, but I must ask you to be frank with me. So far as I know you are the only person on board who was acquainted with this unfortunate lady who is now dead. You have told us that she has relatives in New York, and a son who is dead. You were seen in conversation with her, apparently in intimate conversation since the steward who took your order for drinks saw her holding your arm whilst she spoke to you. Do you still ask us to believe that you met her to-night for the first time?"

"I am sorry," said Benvenuto, getting up, "but it happens to be true. I came across her by accident this morning when she dropped her handbag on the quay, and I picked up her things for her. The facts about herself she told me in the course of our conversation this evening. I am afraid that is all I can tell you."

He bowed to the Captain, who was now standing facing him.

"Just a moment, Mr. Brown," said the inspector, but he got no further; there was a sharp rap on the door; the Captain said "Come in," and there appeared the alert face of Mr. Pindlebury. He came into the room and greeted the Captain.

"Ah! I see you've got hold of him already," he said.

In an instant Benvenuto found himself in the extraordinary position of being surrounded. The Captain had walked swiftly round his desk and was close beside him. On his other side the inspector had closed in, and though he evidently awaited orders his expression was triumphant. Between them, facing Benvenuto, his face creased in a smile that might have been amiable or malevolent, was Mr. Pindlebury, his eye-glass winking at each man in turn.

"I might have known," he said, turning finally to the Captain, "that you'd hit on the right man without *my* telling you. Smart work. Nothing you don't know about your own ship. Well, you won't need me now."

"I shall be very much obliged, Pindlebury, if you'll tell me exactly what you know," said the Captain.

Benvenuto, standing rigid with his back to the desk, looked round at the three faces and wondered if he were losing his reason, or if this were some fantastic nightmare from which he would shortly wake. His first feelings of rage had changed to a condition of amazed curiosity.

"God bless my soul," said Mr. Pindlebury, "don't tell me you know nothing about the last case he was mixed up in? The murder of young Kulligrew in his box at the theatre? Most brutal affair—brutal! He'd have got away with it, too, if it hadn't been for an extraordinary ingenious piece of investigation on the part of our friend here." He raised his hand and patted Benvenuto kindly on the shoulder.

"Investigation—" echoed the Captain. He looked at Benvenuto, then across at the inspector.

"Inspector Markham," he said, "will you kindly wait in the outer office?"

As the door closed behind him, the Captain turned to Benvenuto. "Mr. Brown," he said, "I can only apologize. Now that the Kulligrew case is recalled to me, of course I know who you are. I really am extremely sorry that this should have happened. I—"

A few minutes later, sitting over whiskies and sodas, and with cigarettes alight, the three men began a conference.

At the Captain's request Benvenuto outlined for him, as well as he was able to remember it, his conversation with Miss Smith. When he finished the Captain said:

"In the light of what has since happened, does it not seem to you that the woman was contemplating suicide when she talked with you? Her melancholy, her nervousness, her rather, so far as I can gather, unhinged air—and above all, her vagueness when you mentioned New York—all these things seem to me to point the same way. She had made up her mind to take her own life."

Benvenuto looked at him in a troubled way. "While I agree with you theoretically, I can't feel that you are right," he said. "You see, if she hadn't been found drowned, it would never for one moment have occurred to me that she was in a suicidal frame of mind when she talked to me. And I still don't believe she was. She was wretched, frightened, hysterical, half mad if you like; but she wasn't suicidal. For a moment she seriously considered looking for her sister when she reached New York, until, for some reason, she abandoned the idea. She gave me the impression of someone who had lost her way about life, but who was beginning to take a rather timid interest in it. She was interested in this man Gowling, though whether she recognized his name or not I can't say—I rather fancy she did. She was interested in the length of the voyage. She was excessively interested in the time. She wouldn't have been interested in any of these things if she'd been proposing to chuck herself overboard almost immediately."

"Something in that," remarked Mr. Pindlebury. But the Captain shook his head; to him the affair was plain enough, although the wish was probably father to the thought. A suicide in his ship was bad enough; an accident or a murder was a thousand times worse.

There was a pause. The Captain, erect and impressive in his chair, kept a silence which neither of the other men cared to break. When he spoke, however, he addressed Benvenuto with a certain diffidence.

"The best course appears to me," he said, "to let it be generally understood that this was a case of suicide. My official statement will, of course, contain nothing but the bare facts. Inspector Markham will get to work on the ordinary routine of identification, tracing the relatives and so on—but meanwhile, if you feel inclined to interest yourself in the case, I should feel exceedingly grateful if you would conduct an unofficial inquiry. So long as there exists any element of doubt, it is, of course, my duty to get to the bottom of it. If you care to help me—"

"Certainly, I'll do anything I can," said Benvenuto, getting up. "There is a line I think I may be able to follow, though it is a bit vague at present. Perhaps I could have a talk with Markham to-morrow, and have a look at the body."

The Captain walked with him to the door. "It really is extremely good of you. I'll explain the situation to Markham, and you shall, of course, have every possible facility for your investigations. I consider I am uncommonly fortunate in having you in the ship."

His smile as he shook hands had a sincere and rather bashful quality which stripped him for a moment of his official impressiveness and made him a pleasant, rather worried-looking man.

It was nearly half-past two when Benvenuto reached his cabin. He pushed open his porthole and looked for a few moments at a round framed picture of moonlight on dark water. The sea was in a gentle mood, a vast, oily-black expanse touched with silver; watching it, Benvenuto wished that the vigour of storm and wind would come to disturb its crawling quietness. It seemed to him mysterious, secretive, hiding its strength beneath a smooth-faced calm.

Rather wearily, he took off his dinner jacket for the second time that night, undressed, and climbed into bed. He had a busy day in front of him, he thought as he switched out the light, and must get some sleep.

It was an elusive face. Sometimes he could recall an arched, finely modelled brow, drooping white lids and dark lashes which fell as a tangible veil over that other intangible veil which hung between her eyes and all that she saw. Sometimes, he saw the curve of her lip, or the white line of her chin as she had turned away from him, looking out to sea, whistling her tune; but try as he would, the relation of nose, lip, and chin eluded his memory. The ear met the cheek—so; the slanting eyes were set above high, pale cheekbones—so; and after? He turned over impatiently. He would have to draw her, or paint her, to capture this fugitive beauty of bone and flesh.

By now sleep was as elusive as her image. The tune she had whistled ran through his head as an underlying accompaniment to his restless questioning. Where had he heard it before—what were the words of it? They hovered on the edge of his consciousness and repeatedly escaped him. Insistently, menacingly, the problems of the evening pushed their way to the forefront of his tired mind.

What was the link which connected this strangely assorted group of people—what factor other than chance could have brought them together on this ocean crossing? They ranged themselves before him like figures in some absurd, incongruous masque; Lord Stoke, Leonard Gowling, Morton-Blount, Lady Stoke; the troubling, the elusive Ann; and lastly, the fusty black figure of Miss Smith, whose death had turned the incongruous masque to tragedy. Was she the central figure, was her death the key to this curious conjunction of personalities? Did Ann know of the coming of this death—know of it and desire it?

With unreasoning conviction, he felt a blank refusal to accept this, felt, too, a certainty that the presence of the dead woman was purely incidental; her suicide, or her murder, was the finale to some dark and gloomy story, but it was not Ann's story, it explained nothing.

All logical reasoning had left him in this unreal state between sleeping and waking. He lay in his bed while doubts and questions battled against his instincts and convictions. Gradually as he drifted towards unconsciousness, the sorrowful face of Ann became more real to him. It was sensitive and fine and delicate—it had no place in the story of the dead woman. Faintly her tune followed him, then all at once the words were there, words which troubled his sleep and seemed to cast, once more, dark shadows across the face of Ann:

> Hey nonny no!
> Men are fools that wish to die!
> Is't not fine to dance and sing
> When the bells of death do ring?
> Is't not fine to swim in wine,
> And turn upon the toe,
> And sing hey nonny no!
> When the winds blow and the seas flow?
> Hey nonny no!

THE SECOND DAY

CHAPTER VI
WANTED ON VOYAGE

BENVENUTO'S mood when he woke was singularly at variance with the morning. A beam of sunlight, taking aim through the porthole of his cabin, alighted on his eyelids and roused him to consciousness of an aching head, velvet teeth, and a sensation of having emerged from a darkly foreboding dream-world into an equally dark reality. He climbed slowly out of bed and crossed to the porthole.

Dark reality? The morning was fresh and brilliant, the air light and cool, and possessing an ineffable purity only possible at sea. He took a deep breath and let his eyes wander over an infinity of sparkling blue water and a sky innocent of clouds. Somewhere close at hand a seaman, polishing brasswork, was humming a song below his breath.

Benvenuto's face, tingling in the sunlight, gradually became cheerful. The black vapours of the night were driven away and replaced by a rising elation. Yesterday's tragedy, with its surrounding complications and mysteries, assumed the proportion merely of an interesting problem that would occupy him during the remaining four days of the voyage, and one that would incidentally entail making the further acquaintance of Ann Stewart.

Whistling, he went along to his bath, and during the delightful processes of a fresh-water scrub, followed by immersion in hot, greenish sea-water, and then a cold shower, he had so far recovered his normal balance as to consider the probable arrangement of his paintings on the walls of the New York gallery. He rubbed his lean body, still tanned by the sunlight of the South of France, and decided he would spend half an hour in the gymnasium before breakfast, as the final antidote to a bad night.

A few minutes later, dressed in flannel trousers and a blue sweater, he went out on deck. The *Atalanta's* passengers, save for a couple who were striding purposefully along under the influence of a notice which read 'Five times round this deck is one mile,' were still invisible, and Benvenuto enjoyed his first cigarette in delicious solitude, leaning over the rail and watching the creaming water of the ship, and a determined trail of seagulls which floated above. He was stirred to action by a feeling of hunger, and went down to the deck below to take his before-breakfast exercise.

The gymnasium, bristling with every modern contrivance, from electric slimming belts to the mechanical horses designed for sullen-livered old gentlemen, was deserted except for a white-uniformed attendant, who hurried forward and persuaded Benvenuto into sampling the delights of an electric back-slapper. Soon his body was tingling from contact with its brisk mechanical fingers, fingers which raced up and down his spine with inhuman precision. Suddenly he stood upright, leaving them to batter the air, his interest focused on two people who had just entered.

The first was a cherubic gentleman in a passionately striped dressing-gown, the second a gentleman's gentleman, tall and dark in a romantic manner, and of an elegant slenderness and pallor. But it was the owner of the dressing-gown who held Benvenuto's attention, the stout, pink, and smiling man who shed his gaily-coloured covering on to the arm of his valet, and advanced jauntily towards a mechanical horse. In spite of his benevolent expression he was singularly repulsive, thought Benvenuto, as he watched him swing a chubby leg over the saddle; his flesh was clean and even pink, his costume a brief white vest and shorts, and his small, shining blue eyes protruded from his fat, perpetually smiling face. He resembled an obscene baby astride a hobby horse, a baby who turned suddenly fretful as his horse was put in motion by the attendant.

"Not so fast, damn you," he barked, clutching at the reins, his body a wildly trembling jelly.

"I beg your pardon, my lord," returned the man civilly, adjusting the speed. Then Benvenuto realized that the choleric rider was Lord Stoke; he caught a last glimpse of him from the doorway as he went off to breakfast, an absurd figure bumping slowly up and down in the saddle, flanked on the one side by the grave-faced valet, on the other by the gymnasium attendant, over whose heads his lordship's persistently benevolent smile shone forth with renewed good will. A nasty fellow, decided Benvenuto, and turned his thoughts to eggs and bacon.

Soon his thoughts materialized into rashers crisp as silk, and eggs like suns, fragrant coffee and a dish of fruit. The *Atalanta*, he decided, was a superb hotel, and if the somewhat exuberant decorations were a necessary accompaniment to excellent food, well, they could be borne with fortitude. The dining-saloon was fairly empty—he could see none of his new-made acquaintances, and finished his breakfast in a satisfactory solitude. Perhaps he had time for a book and a deck chair before he need set his mind to the day's problems. He strolled along to his cabin in search of "Candide." As he went in he saw, conspicuous upon his dressing-table, a note:

"DEAR MR. BROWN," he read,

"Could you come along and see me after breakfast? I shall be in my office from nine till ten, and should be glad to discuss a few matters with you. Rather a curious incident has occurred this morning which I think may interest you.

"Yours sincerely,

"GEORGE BECKWORTH."

Benvenuto looked at his watch; it was a few minutes after ten. He abandoned his idea of a deck chair, and after making his appearance a little more formal, went along to the Captain's office.

"Good morning, Mr. Brown." Sir George Beckworth half rose from his chair and shook hands with Benvenuto across his desk. "Sleep well? Splendid! I didn't. Some queer things have happened in my ship since I've been in command of her, but I've never before had a homicidal maniac aboard. Just take a look at this before we get on with last night's business." He slid a letter across the desk, and leaning back rubbed the tip of his nose with the bowl of his pipe.

Benvenuto unfolded the note and saw that it was crudely printed on ship's stationery. It read:

"You traitor. You know why I am here. Your own conscience has told you that. But there is something you don't know for all your Power and Riches. There is a Plot to murder you before we get to New York, and I am the only one in the know. So you have got to see me now and give me my Rights or I will let them kill you. *Think what has happened already.*

"Give me my Rights and I will save you. If not, you will be Done to Death."

"And to whom," asked Benvenuto, "was this letter sent?"

"To someone I can't afford to have murdered in my ship. An important man. I'll go further and say, a self-important man. Why the devil can't they murder each other on land?"

He lit a match and puffed irritably, then looked at Benvenuto through a cloud of smoke with eyes that were a bright and fiery blue.

"He brought me this damn' blackmailing letter—and talked to me as if I were a damn' policeman! On my own bridge." The Captain's hand came down with a bang on to his desk.

"And does Lord Stoke know who sent him the letter?" asked Benvenuto quietly.

The Captain stared; then laughed. "No, he doesn't. Or says he doesn't. Wants me to find the fellah and put him in irons. How did you know it was Lord Stoke, hey?"

"A happy guess. Give me a few hours and perhaps I'll guess the sender. Perhaps not. But will you leave it to me for the moment, sir?"

"I certainly will. I'm delighted to. By the way, I haven't mentioned this to Markham. Thought I'd speak to you first."

Benvenuto nodded. "I think, in this business, I can work better alone, if you don't mind. A certain discretion—"

"You're right. Absolutely. Markham will do any routine work you want, but we can't have passengers' finger-prints taken, or anything of that sort. I tell you, Mr. Brown, it's easier to offend passengers than to swallow a whisky peg. Sometimes I'd rather be in command of a coal tramp out of Cardiff than have to load up with all these tender feelings. Like egg-shells, sir! Like egg-shells. Well, let's have Markham in and get this Miss Smith business over." He rang the bell.

Markham entered with a certain ponderous elegance, his large body and small feet giving him the air of a *maître d'hôtel* about to present the menu to a favoured client. He did, in fact, produce a sheet of paper and lay it before the Captain, who glanced at it and handed it to Benvenuto. It read:

"Unable trace identity Miss Smith stop booked passage Sept. 3rd main office stop have put matter in hands Scotland Yard to investigate through passport and advertised for relatives in press stop will communicate developments stop"

"From our London office," said the Captain. "Nothing to be done, I suppose, till we hear again."

"Perhaps Inspector Markham will take me down to see the body, and the cabin," suggested Benvenuto.

"Of course. Take Mr. Brown along, Markham. Let me know how you get on."

Once outside the door Inspector Markham became artic-
ulate. "Body or cabin first, Mr. Brown?" he inquired, walking beside Benvenuto down the corridor. "I've seen them
both, and what I think will keep till you've come to your
own conclusions."

"Body," replied Benvenuto. "It's more orthodox. By the
way, did she say anything before she died?"

"Not a word. Unconscious to the end. Heart gave out. And
if you ask me there's precious little to go on. Her handbag
and papers went overboard with her, apparently."

In the sick-bay they were joined by the medical officer
who led them into a small room opening off the ward. Here
on the bed, covered with a white sheet, lay a thin still body.

Benvenuto stepped forward and gently drew back the
sheet. For a moment he scarcely recognized the delicate
face as that of the woman in black he had talked to the night
before.

It was Miss Smith; but the waxen pallor of death had
changed her to a fragile Madonna. Now, she looked twenty
years younger; and he realized that once she had been pretty, with that Early Edwardian prettiness that we now find so
perversely attractive. She belonged to the bicycle age, the age
of bell skirts and tiny waists, high sleeves and straw boaters.
"Daisy, Daisy, give me your answer, do!"

With an effort he brought himself back to listen to the
doctor.

"Contusions on left shoulder and side consistent with
striking the water from the height of the boat deck," he
was saying. "Nothing else—no signs of violence. Suicide, if
you ask me. Or accident; though that's hardly likely. Bad
heart; *might* have fainted and fallen overboard."

"Not unless she was leaning pretty far over the rail," put
in Markham. "And even then—"

"Quite," replied the doctor. "Suicide, of course. Clear case. A bit dippy, anyway to judge by her clothes which are about twenty years old. Odd affair."

"What's odder still," said Benvenuto, who had been examining the black water-stained garments, "is that these clothes haven't been worn more than once or twice. They've been packed away—for twenty years—" He was silent, remembering suddenly the smell of moth balls.

"She may have been in prison," suggested Markham. "That would explain it."

"Not prison, I think," said Benvenuto. "Look at her hands. No sign of prison work on *those* finger-tips. 'Stone walls do not a prison make'—at least, not always."

"Well, she'll be identified sooner or later," said Markham. "Meanwhile—the doctor says it's all consistent with suicide. Who'd want to do in a crazy old woman, anyhow? With all due respect to *you*, Mr. Brown, I don't see you've got the slightest evidence to suggest foul play. Have you now?"

"Not a splinter," admitted Benvenuto. "Let's go and see her cabin. After all, who'd want to do in a crazy old woman?"

The ship's engines throbbed to the tune of:

"Daisy, Daisy, I'm half crazy
All for the love of you—"

How did it go on?

"It won't be a stylish marriage—"

Benvenuto stopped. "Just a minute," he said, and re-entered the mortuary. He raised the woman's left hand and looked at the ring finger attentively, then sighed and rejoined Inspector Markham.

Miss Smith's cabin, on the lower deck, was a small one, and contained, beyond the amenities provided by the company, nothing but a medium-sized imitation leather suit-case, quite new and labelled 'Wanted on Voyage' an old umbrella with a long handle, and, quite surprisingly, Huxley's "Brave New World."

Having been assured by Markham that the suitcase represented Miss Smith's entire bag and baggage, Benvenuto opened it, and began to lay the contents out on the bed.

On the top was a layer of coarse calico under-clothes, very clean, but of a texture that made Benvenuto shudder. Beneath lay some black cotton stockings, neatly rolled and bearing little tabs with the lettering 73 marked on each. Then came something soft which gave to his fingers, and revealed itself as a grey feather boa; as he shook it out it exuded into the cabin a sharp reminder of the dead woman with its frowsy camphorated smell. Next came the current copy of *Vogue*, curiously out of place with its chic smartly drawn cover, and lastly, at the bottom of the case, a large package wrapped carefully in newspaper, a newspaper dated, he noticed as he unfastened the pins which held it, a week ago. Under the newspaper covering lay a mass of tissue paper, smooth and immaculate; within it was a perfectly new and very expensive-looking evening gown.

Benvenuto held it up in front of him and stared at it. The flat white crêpe was beautifully cut—Patou he thought at a guess—and fell in elegant folds to the floor. The back was cut down almost to the waist, and across the shoulders fluttered a wisp of the material, half cape, half epaulettes, very gay and smart as it hung from his fingers. Oh, Daisy—Daisy—

His thoughts were interrupted by a roar of laughter from Markham.

"The late Miss Smith was off her rocker, that's obvious," said the Inspector when he could speak. "Even *I* know enough about women's clothes to realize what that frock would look like complete with feather boa and black stockings. A mental case."

Benvenuto glanced up. "I believe," he said, "that she was perfectly sane. A mistaken optimist if you like, but quite consistent. Something glorious was going to happen to her, and she was preparing for it. Look at that frock—it was part of her brave new world. Only she didn't quite know the rules. She was lost—but saw a light in the darkness. She did not commit suicide, Markham. The frock proves it—to me."

Inspector Markham stared at him, and seemed as though he were about to laugh again. However he controlled himself, his face purpling slightly with the effort. He was, after all, under the Captain's orders to assist this misguided amateur. He looked at Benvenuto with half-veiled pity.

"Well, Mr. Brown," he said, "if you can read all that into a flash evening dress, you can see further than I can, and I've been at this job for twenty years. But still, you go your way, sir, and I'll go mine, and if there's anything I can do to help, you've only to ask me. Now I think if you've seen all you want to see, I'll be getting back to my office. I've got some work to do this morning. If you care to go on looking round for a bit, perhaps you'll send the steward along to me with the key when you've finished."

"I will, Markham, and thanks very much."

Benvenuto sat down and lit a cigarette; the smell of moth balls was getting on his nerves. Then he crossed to the dressing-table and stood looking gloomily at the few toilet articles. A box of cheap powder; a pink puff with a china doll's head perched on it; a celluloid comb and a wretched varnished wood hair-brush. From Woolworth's, all of them, he decided. He turned back to the bed, on which the dress lay in arrogant grace. It reminded him of sleek, bored ladies dancing languidly at Quaglino's; of first nights; of mannequins strolling through dress parades. He raised it carefully, and opening the wardrobe placed it on a hanger. Who would claim it, he wondered. What would Miss Smith's next-of-kin make of it? Alas, poor Daisy.

His usually good-humoured looking face was set and grim as he began gently to pack the dead woman's clothes in her suit-case. The coarse cotton under-garments, he noticed, as he smoothed them between his hands, were patched and darned with meticulous care, sewn with small delicate stitches worthy of the finest silk. She had been an idealist, he thought; whatever her life had been, however sordid and confined her surroundings, she had preserved her ideal of beauty and elegance. Looking down at a square of darning that was woven into the coarse material he understood a most gallant integrity of purpose which had led her finally to the purchase of the fine white gown. Who was it who had cheated her of her brave new world? Who, in this ship, could have found it necessary to end her drab existence?

Sitting down on the bed he pulled from his pocket the anonymous letter and read through for the second time its crudely worded threats.

"So you have got to see me now and give me my Rights or I will let them kill you."

"Think what has happened already—"

Coming to a decision he folded the letter and put it in his pocket-book. He would go and have a talk with Lord Stoke. By the exercise of tact, he thought, he might succeed in getting some clue to the writer's identity from his choleric lordship. It might not, probably would not, cast any light on the case of Miss Smith, but at least it was better than inaction. Besides, he thought rather ruefully as he went out of the cabin and locked the door, the Captain had enlisted his aid in soothing his most important passenger's ruffled feelings. Judging by the impression he had gathered earlier in the day in the gymnasium, his lordship would be a difficult man to tackle, and his spirits rose slightly at the prospect. He felt very much inclined for action of some kind after his half-hour in Miss Smith's cabin.

He went up in the lift, and after a momentary hesitation, turned along a corridor. It was temporarily deserted, most of the passengers being engaged in tennis or deck quoits, or in the more peaceful occupation of sipping cups of soup in their deck chairs. So far he hadn't been very successful in following his own ideal of complete idleness, thought Benvenuto, as he approached Lord Stoke's door.

He had, however, little time for regret, for at that moment the door opened and his lordship appeared, and seemed, to Benvenuto's astonished eyes, to be on the verge of apoplexy. His fat face was distorted and purple with rage, and he held in front of him the cringing figure of a small man, and was engaged in shaking him by the shoulders rather as a big mastiff shakes a rat. Both men were perfectly silent, and then suddenly Lord Stoke, loosening his grip on the small man, shot out his right fist into a sickening impact with the other's face, and disappeared into his cabin with a bang of the door. The small man, having been hurled across the corridor with considerable velocity, was lying in a crumpled heap on the floor, and Benvenuto, hurrying forward, bent over him and turned him face upwards.

It was Mr. Gowling.

Dishevelled and battered, his hair on end and his tie under one ear, the little man lay unconscious with a stream of blood beginning to ooze from his lip.

Benvenuto looked round. By some miracle there was still no one in sight, and taking a swift decision he tried the handle of the door immediately behind Gowling's body. It gave to his touch, and after a glance inside Benvenuto picked up the unconscious figure in his arms, and carrying him in dumped him down on the bed. The cabin was untenanted, and Benvenuto, after loosening Gowling's collar, hurried to the wash-stand, dipped a towel in cold water and commenced to bathe Gowling's face. The damage, he could see, was slight, amounting to nothing more serious than a badly cut lip, and after a few moments Gowling's eye-lids began to flutter and he stirred uneasily. Benvenuto took the towel and went back to the wash-stand. Standing quite still he watched the figure on the bed.

Mr. Gowling jerked up with a convulsive movement, then sank back upon the pillow. Half articulately he broke into tearful speech.

CHAPTER VII
FORMULA

"Swine!" sobbed Mr. Gowling. "Dirty cruel swine. They shall get you for this."

His face, a pallid background for blood and tears, was twisted with weak fury. Suddenly he saw Benvenuto, who bent over him, cloth in hand. He shrank away, fingers plucking at his bleeding lip. "'Oo are you?" he whispered.

Instead of answering Benvenuto mopped at the cringing face with cold water, and then gave him a drink. In some disgust he looked down at the trembling figure whose teeth rattled noisily against the glass.

"Thanks," said Mr. Gowling thickly, handing it back to him. Already his lip was beginning to swell. "I seen you before," he went on, looking at Benvenuto suspiciously. Then: "'Ow did I get in 'ere?"

"As a matter of fact I brought you in," said Benvenuto. "My name's Brown. We met last night—Mrs. Stewart introduced us if you remember. I just happened to be passing as you were—er—saying good-bye to Lord Stoke."

The name acted as an immediate stimulus to Mr. Gowling, who sat up. "He's a swine," he repeated shrilly, "a filthy, wicked swine. If you knew what 'e'd done to me—"

"Tell me about it," said Benvenuto, sitting down and pulling out his cigarette case. "Perhaps I could help you." But Mr. Gowling got unsteadily to his feet and took a nervous step towards the door.

"I must be getting along," he said. "Very decent of you, old man, to patch me up, and thanks a lot. Fact is, Lord Stoke's a—a friend of mine and we'd had a few words about a private matter. Nothing serious. His lordship's a bit hasty sometimes. I'm quite O.K. now, so I'll be going."

But Benvenuto was before him at the door. "Go back and sit down," he said quietly. "I've got some questions to ask you."

"Wot's all this?" cried Mr. Gowling, with a mixture of fright and anger. "You can't keep me 'ere. I ain't done nothing. I'm an honest man, I am—which is more than you can say for some people in this blarsted boat. You can't touch me. You be careful. I could buy the 'ole boat up if I 'ad my rights. Stand away from that door."

"In that case," said Benvenuto, reaching out his hand to the bell, "perhaps you'll explain yourself to the ship's detective."

But before he could ring, Mr. Gowling was clutching at his sleeve. "'Arf a minute," he said. "'Arf a minute. Per'aps I was a bit 'asty. We don't want any trouble now, do we? Wot is it you want anyway?"

"That's better," said Benvenuto. "Suppose we both sit down. Have a cigarette. No? Ah yes, I see. I suggest you continue to apply this towel dipped in cold water. Here you are. Now, Mr. Gowling, please don't run away with the idea that I'm either a blackmailer or an inquiring busybody. I've been asked by the Captain to make some investigations for him, and if you will answer a few questions, I've no doubt you can help me a great deal. If not—well, I shall have to turn you over to Inspector Markham. Take your choice."

All the bluster had gone out of Mr. Gowling. He sat nervously on the edge of a chair mopping at his injured lip, and addressed himself with plaintive eagerness to Benvenuto.

"I've got nothing to hide, old man—reely, I haven't. I've come on this voyage for—for my health, and I 'appened to run into my old pal Lord Stoke—known him all my life, we come from the same part, see? And then, well, we had a bit of an argument—not about anything important, I assure *you*—when all of a sudden his lordship lost 'is temper and followed up his words with a blow—and there you are." He attempted to smile ingratiatingly but broke off with a wince of pain. Benvenuto looked at him for a moment in silence and then said:

"If you are as blameless as you say, Mr. Gowling—well, surely you know the penalty of murder well enough to realize that you'd better make a clean breast of everything."

"Murder!" Mr. Gowling sprang from his chair, and his voice was shrill. "I don't know nothing about murder. I don't, I don't. 'Ow dare you say such things! You great bully, you, sitting there trying to frighten an innocent man. Let me out of here!"

Benvenuto put his hand in his pocket and took out the threatening letter to Lord Stoke. He unfolded it and handed it to the frenzied figure in front of him. For a moment he thought Mr. Gowling was about to faint again; instead he collapsed in his chair and burst into noisy weeping. After a pause, Benvenuto addressed him sternly. "Pull yourself together, you little fool, and tell me the whole story."

Gradually Mr. Gowling's sobs subsided, and he raised a twitching face. "I'll tell—I'll tell everything," he quavered. "It's all this manure that's done it—this beastly rotten manure. I've been done out of a fortune, and worried nearly into me grave, and got a sock on the jaw, and now here you come accusing me of murder. Oh dear, oh dear!" He rocked from side to side, clasping and unclasping his hands, then with a final gulp began his story.

"I come from Romley, see—same as Lord Stoke. We was boys together at the same school. He was bigger than me, and 'e always bullied me, and pinched my pocket money. Plain Bill Sutton he was then, the butcher's son. Well, my Dad 'e had a market garden, and a nice little business it was to begin with. Dad was a very superior man with education—he'd been in a chemist's shop when he was young, and he was always full of 'ighfalutin ideas about chemistry and politics and the future of the race. That's what begun all the trouble. Well, Dad got an idea in his head—regular obsession it was— that if only he could make a mixture of the right chemicals or salts or somethin', he could manure the ground so that crops would fair spring up and grow to enormous size. Of course wot 'appened reely was that while he was messing about with his experiments the crops in his own garden got smaller and smaller, and when he died of 'eart failure last year, there was precious little left of the business for *me*. I've been travellin' for some years in Lave-O Soap, but when the old Dad died I threw up me job and went back to the garden. Everything was in a shockin' state—weeds everywhere, and I thought I'd turn it into a tea garden and cyclist's rest. I 'ad a friend in the gin- ger-beer business who was willing to sink a little something in it, and being on the main road I'd soon've made a good thing of it. Oh, dear, oh, dear, 'ow I wish I'd stuck to it—"

For a moment Mr. Gowling was overcome with self-pity, and Benvenuto waited patiently for him to continue. Heav- ing a deep sigh, the little man went on:

"Well, as I was saying, I started to clean the place up, and make it look smart, and one day when I was clearing out the Dad's workshop with a view of giving it a coat of distemper, I came across a little tin of reddish powder up on a shelf, and I chucked it out of the winder on to a patch of grass, and went on with me job. A few days later I went into the work- shop and noticed it seemed all dark and funny like, and then I saw the winder was all overgrown with something green that was blocking out the light. I runs out in the garden, and, believe me or believe me not"—Mr. Gowling's voice dropped to a whisper in his excitement, "that there patch of grass 'ad grown up as high as my chin!

"Well, o' course, I realized what 'ad 'appened. The dream of Dad's life 'ad come true—'e'd got 'is mixture right, and very likely it was the shock of that wot killed 'im. We've always 'ad

brains in our family, and 'ere was proof that Dad was a genius—that's what 'e was, a genius.

"The first thing I thought of when I'd got over my surprise
was that tin of powder, and down I went on me hands and
knees looking for it. That grass 'ad grown up so thick and
strong, it was like hunting through a young forest, and soon I
was fair sweatin' with fright that I shouldn't find it. 'Owever,
find it I did, and there was still some powder left in the bottom, and I sat there on the grass laughin' like a fool, holdin'
the tin in my hands, till suddenly I saw the milkman 'ad come
round and was staring at me. I was just agoing to blurt out
the whole thing, when all at once I realized I mustn't, and I
hid the tin in my coat and sent 'im packing.

"I can't tell you, old man, wot I went through in the next
few days. Imagine my feelings—there I was with a discovery
that meant a fortune in my hands, and not knowing wot to
do with it. I'd take my chair out and sit in the shade of that
bloomin' grass and touch it to remind me it was real, and
wonder what on earth to do. Anyone I told about it might 'ave
robbed me of the secret—I felt like I was sitting on a diamond
mine in me back garden, and if I got up someone would find
out about the diamonds.

"Well, it so 'appened that that week Lord Stoke was coming back to Romley to open the new schools—I ought to 'ave
told you, 'e left home when 'e was a young man, and got rich
and got a peerage too, durin' the war. It seemed to me 'is visit
was the 'and of Fate. 'Ere was just the man I wanted—rich
and powerful, and able to get the stuff examined and made
up, and put on the market for me.

"I managed to talk to 'im, and 'e asked me to come and
see 'im in London and bring the stuff with me. I went up—
and Gawd, I was that frightened there'd be a train smash, or
I'd get run over by a bus before I could get there. 'Owever, I
didn't, and I went to 'is great gilded office and left the stuff
with 'im. 'E was very pleasant, and promised to get the stuff

analysed, and let me know the result. I didn't hear nothing for several weeks, and believe me, old man, I was in 'ell, not knowin' if I was Rothschild or the boss of a tea garden. Just when I couldn't stand it no longer, and 'ad made up me mind to go up to London and see Lord S., a letter arrived. It said—wait a minute—'ere it is."

From an inner pocket, Mr. Gowling brought a dirty and much folded piece of paper, which he handed to Benvenuto. It was typewritten on expensive business notepaper and read:

"MR. LEONARD GOWLING.
"DEAR SIR,
"I am directed to inform you that Lord Stoke has caused the matter of your chemical fertilizer to be examined. The sample has been analysed, and a further quantity prepared, which has been found on experiment to be valueless.
"Yours faithfully,
"PHILIP MULLENS
"SEC."

"Think of it!" almost screamed Mr. Gowling. "Valueless! And me sitting day by day under the shade of that there grass! I wish I'd never laid eyes on the filthy, swindlin' beast."

"What did you do then?" asked Benvenuto.

"There wasn't much I could do," said Mr. Gowling. "First of all I tried to see 'im. I went straight up to the office and asked for him, but I never got further than his high and mighty watchdog of a secretary. Treated me like I was dirt 'e did, and always 'ad 'is answer ready: 'His Lordship was out of town.' 'His Lordship was engaged,' 'His Lordship 'ad nothing further to add to 'is letter.' Swine, the 'ole lot of them, conspiring against me. The next trouble was that I found I was gettin' short of cash—I 'ad no heart for getting to work on the tea gardens with all this 'anging over my head, and I 'ad to get money from somewhere. The upshot of it was I sold the gardens to my friend in the ginger-beer business—'e was a bit surprised, but I didn't explain nothin' to 'im—I'd 'ad enough of giving me secret away. I turned things over in me mind, and decided I'd move to London, so's I could keep an eye on 'is lordship, and when I got there I went to a firm of detectives, and employed them to watch 'im. My idea was that as soon as 'e showed signs of turning my secret into money, I'd go to the police with the 'ole story. You'd never believe wot those detectives run me into—retaining fees, meals, expenses—something chronic it was; by the time they'd got me the information I was pretty near broke again. Robbers, that's what they was."

"And what information did they give you?"

"Jest wot I'd expected." Mr. Gowling hitched his chair closer, his puny face flushed with excitement. "The first thing they told me was that Cyrus Quillan 'ad arrived in London. Maybe you wouldn't 'ave 'eard of 'im—the greatest wheat king of America 'e is, one of the Big Four of the Amalgamated Wheat Combine. The very first day 'e came over 'e 'ad a meeting with Lord Stoke—a private meeting, mind, round at the Metz Hotel where Quillan was staying, not even a secretary with them. Then 'e goes down and stays in Lord Stoke's place in Surrey—and a few days after 'e'd left for America, what do I 'ear but that Lord Stoke is sailing on this boat to attend an important conference of the Wheat Combine in Chicago.

"I didn't know *what* to do; I was pretty near out of cash by that time, and I thought to meself, if I went to the police, either they wouldn't believe me, or if they did and managed to get my secret back from Lord S., it wouldn't be a secret no longer—the formula would be made public, and any bloomin' chemist could make up the stuff and sell it over 'is counter. Then—I 'appened to come up against Mr. Morton-Blount, and feeling desperate, I told 'im the 'ole story."

"Why did you hit on him in particular?" asked Benvenuto.

"Well," Mr. Gowling's face assumed a half-shamefaced, half-cunning air. "'E's a Socialist. That's to say, 'e doesn't believe in trade—*you* know; 'e 'ates Lord Stoke because 'e employs thousands of workmen in 'is factories—calls 'im an oppressor of the poor. Then again, Morton-Blount's got plenty of money, and 'e being a bit soft-like, I knew 'e wouldn't want to make anything out of the secret for 'imself. Also 'e thinks if we can get the secret back, we can use it for the benefit of 'umanity and not for the benefit of Capitalists—and mind you, I wouldn't stand in 'is way so long as 'e gives me a fair price for it. I don't want to take no bread out of the mouths of the poor, I'm sure.

"Well, as I was saying, we 'adn't got much time because Stoke was sailing in a few days. So we decides to come over on this boat with 'im, and 'ave the matter out during the voyage. Morton-Blount bought two tickets, me 'aving no money—though, mind you 'e naturally looks on it like an investment, otherwise I wouldn't 'ave been beholden to 'im. It give us a fair turn when we found Lord S. wasn't on board at Southampton—but luckily 'e turned up on a little motor boat with 'is fancy wife. We were going to arrange a meeting with 'im to-day or tomorrow, but I thought I'd 'ave a quiet talk with 'im on my own, and make 'im see reason before Morton-Blount started putting '*is* oar in. I'd rather you didn't mention it to Morton-Blount, if you don't mind, as 'e might get 'old of a wrong idea 'bout me going be'ind 'is back. Not that I was—I wouldn't think of such a thing. I just thought to save 'im trouble."

"Instead of which you got into trouble yourself."

"I never thought 'e'd turn nasty like that, the dirty brute," said Mr. Gowling wrathfully. "Just shows what a man will do when 'e knows 'e's in the wrong. I was perfectly willing to be reasonable, and listen to any proposal 'e 'ad to offer me—and all 'e did was to give me a sock on the jaw."

"Rude of him," said Benvenuto, "but I daresay he was annoyed by your note. What did you mean about this plot to murder him?"

"Oh, that," said Mr. Gowling, in some confusion. "That was all me eye and Betty Martin. I just wanted to give 'im a fright."

"I see. And where exactly," asked Benvenuto, with an effort, "does Mrs. Stewart come in on all this?"

"She? She's got nothing to do with it—nothing at all," said Mr. Gowling. "She's just a friend of Blount's. I reckon 'e's sweet on 'er, though 'e don't realize it," he added, with rare intelligence.

Benvenuto lit a cigarette. "Take my advice, Mr. Gowling," he said, after a pause, "and don't go sending any more threatening letters, or you'll get yourself into worse trouble still. As it is, you've succeeded in making yourself a bit conspicuous to the authorities over last night's affair."

"Last night?" Gowling looked at him in bewilderment. "I didn't do nothing last night—leastways, if I did see 'er undressing, wot's the 'arm? She never saw me."

"I wasn't referring to Lady Stoke, but to Miss Smith!" said Benvenuto.

"Miss Smith?" The echo was one of blank amazement. "I don't know no Miss Smith."

"Perhaps you knew her under another name," said Benvenuto. "I mean, of course, the poor woman who went overboard last night."

"I 'eard something about it—but wot's it got to do with me? *I* don't know nothing—'ere—are you suggesting—" Mr. Gowling had risen to his feet, and his voice was shrill with indignation.

"I'm suggesting nothing. I simply want you to tell me what you know about her."

"I tell you I *don't* know anything about 'er. You're mad—balmy, that's wot you are, trying to drag me into this. Can't you leave me alone? You've gone and got all me private affairs out of me, and as if that wasn't enough, 'ere you go trying to mix me up with a corpse. I won't 'ave it—I tell you I won't 'ave it. I'm going out of 'ere."

"You make it very difficult for me, Mr. Gowling. I wish you'd sit down and be reasonable. Considering the late Miss Smith recognized you before she died, what could be more natural than my asking you for information about her?"

"Recognized—*me*?" Mr. Gowling's voice was a thin whisper, and he dropped back into his chair. "She can't 'ave done—it ain't true. She was lying," he went on more vigorously—"lying, that's what she was. Just another of them conspiring against me, trying to get me into trouble—oh, dear, oh, *dear!* Why, of course it's lies—I don't know who she was—I've never seen her in me life."

Benvenuto raised his eyebrows. "If you've not seen her, how do you know she wasn't somebody you knew?" he asked.

Mr. Gowling rubbed his head and groaned. "Well, I suppose that's true," he said. "More trouble—nothing but trouble."

"We can soon settle it," said Benvenuto. "Will you come along with me and see if you can identify her? Nobody else on board seems to have known her, and you may be able to save the officials a lot of work."

"Well, if I must I must," he said unwillingly, "but I can't say I like the idea."

As they came out of the cabin, Mr. Gowling looked nervously across at Lord Stoke's door and edged close to Benvenuto. However, all was quiet, and from the unnatural emptiness of the ship it appeared that the passengers were at lunch. In a few minutes Benvenuto entered the antiseptic atmosphere of the ship's hospital for the second time that day; Mr. Gowling, a battered and timid figure, at his heels. After a word with the stewardess in charge, they went along to the quiet room, where the narrow bed held its pathetic, sheet-covered burden. Benvenuto turned back the sheet which rested over the ivory pale face and looked at the man beside him. He put out his arm, but he was too late.

Mr. Gowling had fainted again.

CHAPTER VIII
'WHAT HAD HE TO DO WITH HER?'

"SORRY I'M LATE," said Benvenuto, sitting down in the rapidly emptying dining-saloon. "Give me some hors d'œuvres and—let me see—chicken liver and rice sounds good. And then a salad—how about fresh lettuce with a cheese dressing? Right! And a pint of beer."

He sat back and waited hungrily. It was after two o'clock, and though he had done little since breakfast but listen to the revelations of Mr. Gowling, he had acquired a fine sea-born appetite. Most of the tables were deserted and stewards moved between them bearing trays loaded with the ruins of a thousand meals. But at one table some distance from his own, two people sat engrossed over their coffee cups.

Judging by their attitudes, neither Ann nor Morton-Blount were giving a thought to the absent Gowling, for Morton-Blount, his hair a dark plume over his pale forehead, was gesturing emphatically over some printed matter he held in his hand, and from which he was apparently reading aloud, while Ann's head was bent towards him, and the smoke of her neglected cigarette rose from her fingers in a slim blue column.

Selecting anchovies, olives, and tomato salad from the varied foods beside him, Benvenuto recalled Gowling's remark: "I reckon he's sweet on her—though he don't realize it."

Was Morton-Blount wooing her with pamphlets, praising her beauty in expounding his beliefs? Benvenuto stared broodingly at them. They seemed to his prejudiced eyes so curiously ill-assorted; Ann, with her cool unaffected sophistication, her chic, her abstracted grace. He remembered, comfortably, her half humorous, wholly tolerant expression as she described Morton-Blount's character, remembered echoes he had caught of her own melancholy philosophy. No. She was no missionary, no bride for a social reformer. She would be sensitive, he caught himself thinking, to painting.

And yet, he reflected, women when they are in love are so infernally adaptable; he remembered a ballet dancer whose passion for an anthropologist had engendered in her small head a morbid interest in the human skull; a débutante whose sympathy for higher mathematics sprang into being and flourished side by side with her tenderness for a statistician. Surely, he argued with himself, Ann's was immeasurably the finer brain; surely she could not be won by the emotional outpourings of this amateur Soviet. As he watched them, Ann selected a book from the pile Morton-Blount carried, and leaving the table they walked off together.

Benvenuto took a draught of cold beer and attacked his chicken liver. He must, he decided, see Gowling immediately after lunch, before the little man had had time to recover from the shock he had suffered at the sight of the dead woman. It was no ordinary squeamishness that had sent him off in a second faint, he felt sure; but he had been in no condition for further questions, so Benvenuto had left him with a nurse ministering to his damaged lip and reviving him with brandy, and had given orders for a light lunch to be sent to the little man's cabin.

Gowling was not, he decided, a sensitive type save in so far as his own feelings were concerned. Therefore, his emotion on seeing the face of the dead woman might well have been the result of recognition.

It looked, he thought, as he finished his lunch, as though the problem of identification would be less complicated than he had imagined; and if that were the case, he was halfway to a solution, he told himself optimistically.

Before going to Gowling's cabin he strolled along the promenade deck. There was a breeze which cooled the afternoon sunlight with a slight delicious tang of ice, and which had caused the *Atalanta's* passengers, lying upon a closely packed row of deck chairs, to roll their legs in travelling rugs. They lay in serried ranks, motionless, save for occasional hands which fluttered the page of a book or set knitting needles clicking. For the most part they were wrapped in an after-luncheon lethargy and lay with closed eyes, and seemed to Benvenuto's slightly baleful eye to resemble nothing so much as corpses laid out in a mortuary. Yet it might well be the brain within one of these inert bundles whose black activity had sent a woman to drown, had encircled him, Benvenuto, with a network of problems, and might at this moment be planning further mischief. He walked further aft and leant over the rail, the breeze fanning his face.

> "Is't not fine to dance and sing
>> When the bells of death do ring?
>> Is't not fine to swim in wine
>> And turn upon the toe
>> When the winds blow and the seas flow—"

He stared down into the curling water, the words running through his head. For a moment he found himself wishing he had never come aboard, never had to face the problem of Miss Smith, never met Ann Stewart—if his thoughts of her had to be uneasily entangled with some incomprehensible story of violence and death. Why, indeed, he thought peevishly, couldn't people murder each other on dry land instead of intruding upon this pleasant and highly artificial board-ship life with their personal feuds? It seemed to him at that moment like a breach of manners.

Then his thoughts turning once more to Ann, he started off along the deck, knowing that he would get no peace until he had solved the problem of Miss Smith's death. It was a personal and urgent thing with him now—for while he continually refused the admission that Ann could, even passively, have wished the death of the faded solitary occupant of the ship's mortuary, yet in his mind there existed a conviction that Ann was no ordinary placid ocean traveller. She had not come aboard this ship for the sole purpose of crossing to New York.

—"When the winds blow and the seas flow—"

Impatiently he drove the tune from his head, and knocked upon the door of Gowling's cabin.

For a moment there was silence. Then he heard a thud and the sound of feet pattering across the floor. He waited, then knocked again, whereupon the handle turned and the face of Mr. Gowling peered cautiously round the door. His lip was now elaborately decorated with plaster, and his expression when he saw Benvenuto changed from one of extreme trepidation to a scowl of annoyance.

"Oh, it's you," he said.

"I'm afraid it is. May I come in for a moment?"

Mr. Gowling grudgingly opened the door a little wider, revealing himself in a dressing-gown made apparently from the tartan of an unknown clan, and admitted Benvenuto into his cabin. He looked unhealthily pale in his fierce garment, and while one side of his ginger moustache had been trimmed back to allow for his surgical dressing, the other dropped disconsolately, giving him a half sad, half jovial expression.

"I'm not supposed to see visitors," he said querulously. "Rest and quiet, that's what I'm to 'ave." As he spoke he was tumbling some papers into an attaché case which he locked and put aside.

Benvenuto, uninvited, dropped into a chair.

"I shan't keep you long, Mr. Gowling," he said. "I thought I'd drop in and see how you were feeling. It must have given you a bit of a jar."

Mr. Gowling looked at him suspiciously, then sat down and assumed a more friendly expression.

"You're right," he said, "Nasty thing to 'appen to a man, unexpected and all. They tell me," he went on confidentially, "that I was lucky it wasn't worse. Another half inch to the left and I'd 'ave lost me front teeth. I 'ad a bit of a job, explaining 'ow I'd tripped up over a step. Nosy-parkers, them nurses. Lucky it wasn't at night, or they'd 'ave concluded I was in liquor. And that," finished Mr. Gowling emphatically, "is a thing I could *not* abide."

Benvenuto looked at him. Was he being purposely evasive?

"I wasn't referring," he said, "so much to the sock on the jaw, as to the shock you must have had on seeing the dead body of a friend."

Mr. Gowling jumped up as if he had been stung.

"Now, none of that," he said shrilly, clutching his dressing-gown around him with a nervous hand. "I won't stand it, I tell you. I've had enough of your bullying—coming in 'ere after a sick man with your wicked insinuations. You get out. I never saw that woman before in me life, and no amount of brow-beating from you can make me say I 'ave!"

"Why, then, all the excitement?" said Benvenuto, patiently. "You jump to conclusions, Mr. Gowling. I'm not trying to incriminate you. I'm merely trying to establish the identity of this woman, and I was in hopes, after your reaction on seeing her, that you'd be able to help me."

Mr. Gowling licked his lips nervously and sat on the edge of his chair. "It's you that's jumping to conclusions," he said, in a calmer tone. "You go taking a man wot's just been through a very narsty experience, and go bringing him face to face with a corpse—and wot do you expect 'im to do? Shake 'ands with it? I tell you, I never saw that woman before, and if she said she knew me, then she was lying. That's what she was doing—lying."

Benvenuto repressed a violent desire to decorate Mr. Gowling's face with a further injury, and got to his feet. "I assure you that the poor lady did not claim your friendship, in my hearing, at least. I will tell Inspector Markham what you say and leave him to deal with you."

Benvenuto marched out of the cabin with the minor satisfaction of knowing that he had left Mr. Gowling even paler than before, and went on deck. Although usually a peaceable person, those few minutes in the cabin had filled him with almost ungovernable rage and distaste. The only satisfactory method of dealing with Mr. Gowling would be a severe physical chastisement, he thought, and found himself feeling quite sympathetically disposed towards Lord Stoke. Meanwhile this wretched peevish self-centred little coward was proving a serious stumbling block in the way of his investigations. Did he, or did he not, recognize the dead woman? Benvenuto, reconsidering the interview, was unable to make up his mind.

"You look," said a clear voice beside him, "as though life wasn't suiting you so well to-day."

He turned with a start from his frowning survey of the waters, to find Ann Stewart beside him. Ann, very elegant in a big coat of cream wool, looked at him coolly, and with vague amusement.

The sight of her came as a cold shock to him. He had been thinking of her with such intensity, trying to understand her, to reconstruct in his memory her face, the tones of her voice, trying to separate her image from a dark shadow which, he felt, overhung it. Now that she stood beside him, he felt oddly down-cast. She was utterly aloof, impersonal, wrapped in herself. Who was she, what was she? What had he to do with her?

"It is not so much life that doesn't suit me, as death," he said.

Her eyes flew to his face, then away. "What do you mean?" The words came swiftly.

"I mean that I have spent this morning trying to discover something about the drowned woman."

"The drowned woman—" Her voice sounded as though she had forgotten the incident, was trying to recall it.

Benvenuto stared at her, uncomfortable doubts creeping into his mind. Was she acting? He came impulsively to a decision.

"Mrs. Stewart," he said, "will you do something for me? I'm in a bit of a muddle, and I feel if I could talk over this business with someone I might be able to straighten it out. I've been looking at this poor woman's clothes this morning, and I'd like to know if you draw the same conclusions from them that I have. Will you come and see?"

She looked at him hesitatingly. Then: "Of course I will," she said.

CHAPTER IX
'DAISY, DAISY—'

WHEN ANN HAD nothing she wished to say her gift of silence amounted to a talent, thought Benvenuto, walking beside her along the deck. It was more than silence; it was, it seemed to him, a complete withdrawal from her immediate surroundings. He was determining, nervously, to make a remark, when she spoke.

"Why are you interested in this poor creature who committed suicide?"

"Chiefly," said Benvenuto, "because she did not commit suicide. She was murdered."

He held her attention now, so completely that he felt like a conjuror who had brought off a particularly successful trick.

"You are sure?"

"Well, if you put it like that"—Benvenuto rumpled his hair and looked out to sea—"you make me begin to doubt my own convictions, which I refuse to do. Yes," he went on, after a pause, "I think I can say I *am* sure. There are many reasons. For one thing—do you know that people who commit suicide by drowning rid themselves as much as possible of anything superfluous they have about them before jumping in? Odd, but true. Men nearly always take off their coats, women very often leave their frocks behind them. You might argue that Miss Smith being a lady of the old school, wouldn't undress on the boat deck of a liner—but I think we can be *pretty* sure she wouldn't have gone overboard complete with kid gloves, a shawl, and, apparently a handbag. As a matter of fact, this is the least of my reasons. You see, I am the only person known to have talked with her she was indeed having a drink with me on deck half an hour before she went over—and I'm perfectly certain that she had no thoughts of suicide in her head then. Inside this cabin," he paused, took the key from his pocket and unlocked the door, "there are a number of things which seem to me to support my point of view."

He shut the door, drew up a chair for Ann and gave her a cigarette.

"By the way," he said, as he lighted it, "you are now alone in this cabin with a man who at a late hour last night was suspected of having murdered Miss Smith." He smiled at her. "Perhaps that explains my interest in the case."

"You don't have to explain to me now why you are interested," said Ann. "Mr. Pindlebury was telling me about you yesterday evening, and how you spend your leisure in brilliant investigations to help the police."

"Mr. Pindlebury is inaccurate," said Benvenuto. "I have often spent a good deal of time and energy in attempting to outwit the police. Life would be a good deal simpler if one were always on the side of ready-made law and order. Tell me, do you sew?"

"Sew?" repeated Ann.

"Yes—hem, gather, darn—with a needle and thread. You know."

"I sew rather well. Why?"

He bent down and unfastened the suit-case, then taking out a coarse cotton chemise he handed it to her. "Can you sew as well as that?" he said.

She looked at the darn beneath his finger. "It is beautifully done. It is," she hesitated, frowning, "curious to put such work into such material. The repairs are so much finer than the original fabric."

"Exactly!" He took the garment from her hands. "You know, I think that rather describes this woman's life. The repairs—were so much finer than the original fabric. I know very little about her—but may I tell you what I know—and what I guess?"

"Please—" She leant back, smoking her cigarette, calm, poised, and a little indifferent.

"She was, I suppose, something over fifty. She had lain for many years in some obscure backwater of life—for so many years that she herself had lost count of them. Where she had been, what she had been doing, I don't know—but from the evidence of these miserable yet delicately repaired clothes we can guess that she had very little luxury or beauty in her life. Then, by some unexpected event she was released or she escaped from this narrow place where she had been so long, and she started out on an exciting pilgrimage into the world. She was frightened and hesitant, she blinked at the light like someone emerging from a dark room, but she was full of courage, full of a great determination to take part in that life which had been denied her, and to build up something beautiful and bright and elegant on the dusty foundation of her past.

"Can you imagine what her feelings must have been as she dressed herself up in the ancient clothes which she had worn before her captivity, clothes which had been laid aside for twenty years, peered at herself in the glass and went off to buy this powder for her wrinkled face? She was starting on a glorious adventure. Into her bag she packed her clothes—and with them," Benvenuto bent down again to the case beside him, "like talismans, like maps to guide her through a new country, she packed these."

He held out to Ann the copy of *Vogue*, and Mr. Huxley's "Brave New World." Then, for the first time since he had begun his story, he looked at Ann, and hoped that the anxiety he felt did not show in his face. How was she taking his story—how much or how little did it mean to her? But her face was as inexpressive as a mask as she sat there, a new cigarette between her fingers, waiting still and calm for him to continue.

"Please go on," she said.

"Well, there isn't much further to go," said Benvenuto. "Somewhere in this ship is the rest of the story, for it must have been for the purpose of seeking out somebody that she came aboard. She had no clear idea when she talked with me where the ship was heading—but she had one very clear idea in her mind, which was that she had something to do—someone, I think, to meet—between half-past ten and eleven last night. I believe that she met that person, had that interview, which was to mark the real beginning of her pilgrimage, the real beginning of her new life—and I believe that that person sent her to meet, not life, but death.

"Yet she couldn't have been asking very much—just a little freedom, a few of the beautiful and sweet things that existed all round her. I haven't shown you the dress she had bought in which to face her new world."

He got up and went to the wardrobe, then turned to Ann with the white dress hanging from his fingers. She had risen to her feet.

"Poor thing—oh, poor thing!"

She raised her face to Benvenuto's, the hem of the dress in her hands, so that it hung between them, a soft white curve. Benvenuto, his grip tightening ridiculously on the flimsy material, stared at her across the dress, quite speechless with elation and relief as he watched. For the pale, composed mask of her face had crumpled, broken up under his eyes, and instead he saw a very young very troubled human creature, whose mouth quivered in pity, and whose eyes were shining pools of indignant horror. For a moment this cold and distant and secretive woman was a small girl shocked into tears at the sight of senseless and ugly cruelty.

With a quick movement she took the dress from him, held it against her body and stood so for a moment, tears rolling slowly down her face. Then, very carefully she took it and hung it back in its place, with quiet, gentle movements as though she feared to hurt it. Closing the cupboard door she turned and seized Benvenuto's wrist with an intensity, a change of mood, which startled him. There was no softness in her face now; instead, it was set in hard lines of pain, her eyes burning furies in a white pallor. She looked, he thought, like a Goddess of Wrath.

"It must stop. It must stop. You must find him, whoever did this. My God! if I had him here, beneath my hands! You must find him, hunt him down—crush him. *This* is *your* job—you see that? When you find cruelty like this you have to avenge it. It must stop."

He took her hands and sat her down on the bed beside him. He gave her a cigarette and took one himself. She was near breaking point, he thought, every nerve stretched taut and vibrating. A Goddess of Wrath, but a sick goddess.

"It shall stop," he said quietly. 'I'll see to that!"

When he had taken her back to her cabin, he hurried along to the office of the wireless operator. He took a form, wrote:

"Detective Inspector Leech, Criminal Investigation Department, Scotland Yard. Can you trace discharge or escape of woman patient from private mental home during past month after long residence. Age about 50. Tall, thin, dark. Name possibly Smith. Laundry mark 73. Was she

ever resident Romley Kent. Urgent, thanks. Benvenuto
Brown, S.S. *Atalanta*."

It would take more, he thought, handing the form to the
operator and walking out into the sunlight, a good deal more
than Leech's efficiency to get him the information he wanted.
It would take luck as well; but now, for some reason, he felt
extraordinarily optimistic.

CHAPTER X
RACE MEETING

"COVER THE FIVE and the nine. You can't go wrong," murmured Mr. Pindlebury in Benvenuto's ear as he passed him,
pushing his way towards the bookmaker.

In the interval between tea and cocktails the *Atalanta's* passengers had gathered in the Palm Lounge to attend a
race meeting. Upon a long table the green course was laid, a
course highly complicated by fences and water jumps, while
at the starting post stood a line of painted wooden steeds with
numbers large upon their backs. A deplorable looking crew
from an equine standpoint, thought Benvenuto, but each one
served to attract large quantities of the passengers' money.
It seemed the most popular of all ship sports, for round each
bookmaker surged an anxious crowd—old men in white flan-
nels, youths in plus fours, superb young women in the sports
clothes of Chanel and Augustabernard, bejewelled matrons,
all eager to put their money on the first steeplechase. At a
nearby table two over-clean children with over-curled yellow
hair waited, wide-eyed, under the care of the chief steward
to throw the dice which were to settle the fate of the horses.

Benvenuto glanced up at the tote, and decided to put five
shillings on each of Mr. Pindlebury's numbers. Mr. Pindlebury, looking even more horsey than usual, his eye-glass
screwed into place and a race-card in his hand, was engaged
in giving his advice to the slender American blonde whose

painted eyes gazed at him admiringly. Benvenuto watched them with amusement, then felt a little tug at his coat. Turning he saw Mrs. Pindlebury nodding and smiling at him as she dodged about among the crowd. At last she reached his side, a little breathless, and thrust a ten shilling note into his hand.

"Please—would you put it on the Number three?"

"Certainly—but your husband is backing the five and the nine, you know," he said.

"Yes—yes. The Number three, please. Do be quick. It's such a nice animal, much more like a horse than the others. Thank you so much."

She disappeared into the crowd, still smiling and nodding, and Benvenuto had just time to place her bet before the bell rang.

As he took the receipt, a cloud of perfume enveloped him, and turning he saw an extraordinarily beautiful girl whose elaborately dressed red hair surmounted a sulphur-coloured suit. Her fingers with brightly painted nails were crumpling a crisp note which she pushed across the table. "Number seven, please," she said.

"Sorry, madam, the betting is closed."

"Oh, come now, it's only little me," protested the girl.

The steward looked up.

"Very sorry, my lady, but I can't take any more bets on this race."

She turned away, biting her scarlet lips. "Nasty old pig," she muttered, and caught Benvenuto's eye.

He smiled at her, lending his face to an unfamiliar expression of gallantry.

"That's too bad," he said. "I'm in the same boat. I was so busy placing a bet for somebody else that I had no time for my own. Suppose we take a plunge on the next one? You'll bring me luck, I'm sure."

Her ladyship's face cleared and she smiled coquettishly.

"Righto," she said. "How about a little drinky?"

"You have the most marvellous ideas," said Benvenuto, piloting her to a table. He chose a secluded one, behind a palm tree. "What is it to be?"

"Gin fizz for me," she responded, studying her face in a jewelled mirror.

He gave the order to a waiter, then bent towards her. "I've been waiting two years for this afternoon," he said.

"Whatever do you mean?"

"Can't you guess? I've been longing to meet you ever since I saw you in *Kick the Bucket*."

"Oh, go on," said Lady Stoke, pleased.

"I used to go and watch you every night. I tried to paint you once, from memory, but it was no good. Your face is so extraordinarily subtle," he added untruthfully.

"Are you an artist? I know heaps of artists—I made quite a collection of them once. Do you know Maurice Reville? He's a nice boy."

"I know his portrait of you, of course. It doesn't do you justice, you know."

"Don't you think so? That's what Stokey says. He wouldn't buy it in the end. Though between you and me and the ice bucket, it was because he got mad with Maurice for wanting so many sittings. He *did* get a bit fresh, I must say. Wanted to paint me in my birthday suit. The idea! Don't you think it was the limit?"

Benvenuto coughed, recalling swiftly a feast of shapely limbs in the chorus of *Kick the Bucket*.

"Most fearful cheek," he said. "But you can hardly blame him, can you? When I think how marvellous you'd be to paint—"

"There you go! You artists, you're all alike. You've got no respect for a girl even when she's a peeress. It's the artistic temperament, I suppose."

Benvenuto hitched his chair a little closer.

"Don't be angry with me, please. It's your own fault, you know, for being so beautiful. I've got the most tremendous respect for you. I think you're marvellous, to look like a goddess and to behave like one too."

She looked at him uncertainly, then melted into a seductive smile. "All right—if you promise to be a good boy we'll get on fine."

Benvenuto, as if by accident, touched her hand.

"Now, how about another drink—just to show you've forgiven me?"

"O-o, aren't you awful! Well, just a teeny weeny little drink, and then I must run away before Stokey begins looking for me. You've no idea—" she went on, "how jealous that man is. If anyone so much as passes me the butter—"

"Who wouldn't be, in his place?" said Benvenuto gallantly, and signed to the waiter. "Are you staying in New York long?" he asked.

Lady Stoke's brow darkened. "We're not staying at all," she said. "We're going straight through to Chicago. Isn't it enough to make you sick? *I* wanted to stay in New York, but he won't let me. Suspicious old beast. This is a business trip—and if it comes off he's promised me the Lulworth diamonds. Now this is confidential, this is. Do you think they'll suit me?"

"I think you'll look perfectly divine in them," said Benvenuto, "but then you'd look divine in anything. You'll be the envy of every woman alive."

A gleam came into Lady Stoke's eyes, a quite ferocious gleam that made her look, he thought, like a hungry lioness considering its supper. She lowered her lids.

"Well, I haven't got them yet," she said, a moment later, "and it's no good counting your chickens, is it?"

"I suspect they're as good as round your neck already," said Benvenuto. "Your husband's a very clever man, isn't he?"

Lady Stoke smirked. "Well, he generally gets what he wants, I must say. Anyway, he got me—though I led him a dance I can tell you. And if he brings off this stunt—well, he's pretty mysterious about it, but so far as I can make out he'll be able to buy up the little old world if he wants it."

She set down her half-empty glass and looked at him nervously. "I didn't ought to talk about it really—it isn't everyone I'd talk to like this, I can tell you. But I'm sure you can respect a girl's confidences—I always know a gentleman when I see one."

"You honour me," said Benvenuto. "Let us drink to the Lulworth diamonds—and an owner really worthy of them."

"If you mean me," said Lady Stoke archly, "I guess I'll drink too."

She raised her glass to a vision of herself arrayed in the jewels of a dead queen; drank, and set it down empty. Her eyes were soft and amorous as she leant towards Benvenuto. "It's nice us meeting like this, isn't it?" she said.

"For me, it is the most marvellous stroke of luck," said Benvenuto sincerely. "But we ought to have met long ago. You must have been extraordinarily young when you married."

"I've only been married three months, you know," said Lady Stoke. "Not that I'm so long in the tooth yet."

"Really? I don't remember seeing it in the papers."

Her face clouded. "That was Stokey's fault. He's got a lot of influence with the Press, you know. He set his mind on a quiet marriage, and once he's got an idea in his head he's as obstinate as a mule, believe me. Why, he even insisted on a registry office, and I don't think that's hardly good class, do you? I was ever so disappointed—cried my eyes out, I was so set on white and orange blossoms at St. George's. After all, it *is* more virginal, isn't it? But there you are—he's terrible once he gets set on a thing. And jealous! My word! You'd better not be seen around with me too much, you know. I've got one boy friend on board as it is. It's Rutland King—I expect you've seen him already. He's an old friend of mine, though Stokey doesn't know that."

"Rutland King?" repeated Benvenuto.

"Oh, you men! Don't tell me you don't know who Rutland King is—the greatest lover on the screen! There's a boy with S.A. *I* can tell you. He's got on wonderfully since the Talkies came in—he's got ever such a refined voice, not like some of these cheap slobs who made their name on the old silent. Why, Rutland gets the biggest pay-roll in Hollywood. He's a wonderful actor. And he's just crazy about me. Always was in the old days when we were together in variety, though of course he hadn't a dime then. You must meet him—he'd like you, I'm sure, because he's ever so artistic. He'll be about soon—he spends the afternoons in his cabin, reciting Shakespeare. I say, you know, we're forgetting all about the racing. Aren't you awful keeping me here like this? I must have a flutter on a little horsey. Come along now, do."

They edged their way through the crowd just before the start of a race, and this time Lady Stoke was able to place her bet. Benvenuto too, had invested a modest sum on the Number seven when the bell rang and the race began. The two children at the table, self-conscious smiles on their pink and white faces, each threw a dice.

"Number seven, four—" shouted the chief steward, and Lady Stoke gave a suppressed shriek of excitement. Benvenuto watched her in amusement as the race went on. She pressed forward amongst the crowd, her face reflecting vividly the changing fortunes of Number seven. It lagged behind and she scowled and clenched her hands; it successfully passed a water jump and her eyes blazed in fierce triumph. As it neared the finishing post she was tense with anxiety, her lips compressed into a hard line, the pupils of her eyes dark pools in velvet brown, her fingers gripping her hand-bag so that the knuckles showed white. It was no game for her now; she was a born and passionate gambler—and a bad loser too, he judged. But this time she had no need to show her mettle, for Number seven won, and Lady Stoke was the first at the bookie's desk. As her fingers stretched over her winnings, a voice beside her made her start.

"What is this? I don't like to see my little pet gambling."

She turned, her face reddening, her hand clutched tight over her winnings. Her eyes were half frightened, half rebellious, as she turned them up to the man beside her.

"Now, come, Stokey, I was only having a bit of fun. This gentleman brought me here—this is Mr.—er—"

"Brown," said Benvenuto. "How do you do, Lord Stoke!"

His lordship's smile was benevolent, though his small eyes were points of steel. He nodded to Benvenuto, then turned back to his wife and stretched out his hand.

"Now give that to me, little one, and it shall go to the Seamen's Mission. I can't have my little wife gambling. She mustn't do it again." His smile blazed serenely, but his hand closed over his wife's in a grip that was by no means gentle. Benvenuto excused himself and left them there, he bland and steely, she a burning and rebellious fury.

CHAPTER XI
SEX APPEAL

BENVENUTO, finishing his dinner, looked across the crowded saloon and saw that Ann Stewart was leaving her companions at table. He got up and joined her as she walked towards the door.

"I was wondering," he said, "if you'd have coffee and a drink with me."

"I should love to," said Ann, "if you'll promise not to talk about Russia."

"I believe that I can think of several other conversational openings," said Benvenuto, feeling for some reason extraordinarily pleased. "First of all, tell me if you followed my prescription this afternoon, and took a siesta."

"Sleeping isn't one of my vices," she said, "but I spent the afternoon in my cabin reading. Tell me," she went on in a lower voice as they walked up the stairs, "have you got any further—are you any nearer the solution? I have been thinking about that poor creature and her pathetic clothes."

"To tell you the truth," answered Benvenuto apologetically, "I've been having an afternoon off. I may even be said to have got off. I took a lady to the races—and now I come to think about it—I believe you know her. It was the beautiful Lady Stoke."

He looked round in surprise, for Ann had stopped dead and was leaning back against the stair rail, her hand gripping the shining wood.

"*Lady* Stoke—" she repeated softly. "Lady Stoke I didn't know such a person existed."

He was becoming fanciful about Ann Stewart, decided Benvenuto; reading emotions into her face that could not possibly exist.

"Do you know her husband?" he asked.

Ann walked on up the stairs. "I've never met either of them," she said carelessly. "Are they nice?"

"It looks," said Benvenuto, "as if you are about to have an opportunity of judging for yourself. I hope you don't mind?"

For at a nearby table in the lounge Lord and Lady Stoke were seated over their coffee cups, and she was signalling imperiously to Benvenuto with her fan. She looked, he thought, like a Metal Combine, her curling hair a gleaming copper under the electric light, her gown a sheath of gold, and her throat and wrists a white background for elaborately fashioned platinum ornaments. She was radiant, dazzling, and yet somehow macabre in her glittering beauty; a *poule de luxe*—and a peeress.

Benvenuto looked doubtfully at Ann, but she, after momentary hesitation, moved forward.

"I should like—to meet them," she said nervously.

Lady Stoke looked enticingly at Benvenuto and opened her peerless lips.

"Oh, pardon me!" she said. "I didn't know you had a lady friend with you. Won't you both come and have a little drinky? We were feeling ever so lonesome till you came along. Charmed to meet you."

For a moment as the hands of the two women touched they looked at each other, her ladyship with a swift appraising eye which measured every detail of Ann's appearance from the lines of her long slender body in its black frock to the pearls on her fingers; Ann with a strangely serious and penetrating regard as though she wished to see into the secret self concealed behind her ladyship's glittering and youthful façade.

Seated at the table Benvenuto watched in amusement the homage on Lord Stoke's fleshy face as he addressed himself to Ann. His voice took on its oiliest and most genial inflection as he invited her to drink; no wonder, thought Benvenuto, he is a prince of commerce since he can recognize quality so far removed from his own. Then he gave his attention to Lady Stoke, who to his embarrassment was addressing him behind the shield of her fan.

"I think your girl friend is wonderful, really. Just like Greta Garbo, isn't she? That sad look and all. You've got good taste, haven't you?" She turned the battery of her eyes full upon him, and with an effort he pulled himself together for the correct reply.

"Surely I proved that this afternoon," he said.

"O-o-o! There you go. You artists, you're dreadful really. Never let a chance go by, do you? Stokey was ever so cross with me for going to the races with you, too. The woman always pays, as they say, doesn't she?"

With a final melting of the pupils she lowered her fan, and her eyes went hard as they rested on her husband deep in conversation with Ann. She leant across the table.

"I was just telling your friend how much we've been admiring you, Mrs. Stewart," she said. "That's ever such a beautiful gown you're wearing, if you'll excuse my saying so. And your figure! It's enough to make a snake jealous. However do you do it, dear? Not with chocolates, I'm sure. You must think I'm dreadful rattling on like this, but I always believe in saying what I think. It gets me into hot water sometimes, I can tell you. I've always been the same, haven't I, Stokey? I think something—and out it pops!"

Lord Stoke's smile ran in oiled grooves.

"My wife is a little child of nature," he said, "with a child's wilfulness and a child's enthusiasm. Ah! youth, youth! It is a beautiful thing. Perhaps you think I am a foolish old man, sir," he beamed at Benvenuto through the smoke of his cigar, "but I tell you that through all the wear and tear of the world of affairs, I keep my eyes fixed on the simple things of life. The laughter of children—the flowers of the fields—youth—kittens—" His sentence tailed off in a flourish of his cigar. For a moment no one knew what to say. Then Lady Stoke pouted becomingly.

"Really, Stokey, to hear you talk, anyone would think I was still at school. I don't know what my friends will think of you, I'm sure."

"I think," said Ann clearly, "that it is very wonderful of Lord Stoke to preserve his fine ideals."

Benvenuto looked apprehensively across the table. But Lord Stoke had swallowed it whole, and was toasting Ann in his brandy. Lady Stoke's gilded slippers tapped restlessly upon the floor and her shoulders swayed in time to distant music.

"How about taking the child wife for a little dancey?" she suggested. Her husband's glance held the merest hint of impatience, but he rose to his feet. "Youth must be served," he said genially. "Shall we go to the ballroom, Mrs. Stewart?"

Benvenuto, following them towards the music with Lady Stoke beside him, kept his eyes fixed on the two figures ahead and replied somewhat at random to her ladyship's conversation.

To watch Ann walking was an æsthetic delight. How strange and rare, he thought, to find a woman who neither bounced, strutted nor ambled; who did not walk as though each movement of her hips conveyed notice of her charms to the onlookers; or again, as though she were practising an unfamiliar and rather painful method of getting from one place to another. Ann walked with a slow careless grace, effortless and light, so that, watching the delicate and perfect balance of her movement he caught again his first impression of her, as if she moved, barefoot, across a lawn.—"No," he said to Lady Stoke, "as a matter of fact, I've never been to the Ace of Spades in my life. What does one do there—?"

Ann's head was bent slightly, for the top of Lord Stoke's shining head didn't come much above her shoulder. They were going to look rather peculiar together on the dance floor, thought Benvenuto. What was she saying to put his lordship in such spirits? The rolled flesh at the back of his neck was oozing dangerously over his coat collar as he gave a gust of laughter.

"—four o'clock in the morning," Lady Stoke's voice went on confidentially, "and there was Stokey asleep in the Rolls with a bottle of bubbly in his arms. You would have *screamed*— O-o, look!" She clutched his arm suddenly, "that's Rutland standing in the doorway. Isn't he too divine?"

Benvenuto looked, and saw leaning against a gilded pillar a young man in an attitude of Byronic melancholy, a young man whose face had looked down at him, larger than life-size, from the façade of a thousand picture palaces. To give Rutland King his due he was uncommonly good-looking, thought Benvenuto, and if his expression registered to an almost unreasonable degree a romantic melancholy towards the world in general, well, no doubt it filled the box-office and set up sympathetic vibrations in countless female hearts. His gloom lifted slightly as he caught sight of Lady Stoke.

"Sylvia," he murmured, and kissed her hand.

"This," said Lady Stoke, "is Mr. Brown. I'm sure you'll like him because he's so artistic. You must let him paint you, darling."

"How do you do!" said Rutland King sadly. "I am glad to meet a fellow artist in this Philistine atmosphere. One's life is a perpetual torture, don't you find?"

"As a matter of fact, I rather enjoy life on a liner," said Benvenuto. "Have a cigarette," he added hurriedly, with an obscure idea of comforting this afflicted creature.

"Thanks a lot," murmured Rutland King in his exquisitely cultured tones. He produced a platinum lighter from his pocket and applied it to Lady Stoke's cigarette, while their eyes met over the tiny flame. Benvenuto repressed an instinct to interrupt them as he caught sight of Lord Stoke on the edge of the dance floor. He was staring at his wife out of a rapidly purpling face, and he suddenly relinquished his hold on Ann, with whom he was dancing, and hurried across the floor.

"Sylvia!" he barked sharply.

Benvenuto, with a murmured apology, joined Ann and swept her into the midst of the dancers.

"That was a noble deed," said Ann. "I was just wondering whether to do a pas seul."

"It would have been pleasant," said Benvenuto, "to punch his head—though distinctly ungrateful, since I owe this dance to him. I'm most frightfully sorry to have caused you to meet such a bounder."

"Don't apologize. I've been finding him extremely interesting. But why did he so suddenly abandon me?"

"I think he was alarmed at seeing his wife melting under the eye of the world's most famous lover. Do you realize I've just been introduced to Rutland King?"

"Oh! Do you—do you think Lady Stoke is in love with him?" inquired Ann hopefully.

"With her husband, d'you mean?"

"No, no. Of course not. Oh—you don't think she could be in love with *him*, do you?"

"I understand," said Benvenuto, "that the female crocodile frequently falls in love with the male crocodile. It's a little difficult to put oneself imaginatively into her position. I should think the chances are, Lady Stoke has chosen a perfect mate. I say, don't let the Stokes spoil this dance—"

"But I want to understand," said Ann. "You see, she—she interests me enormously. She seems to me completely unreal—yet how can one be sure she isn't a real human being, like oneself—"

"I should think she's got a number of real passions pretty highly developed, if that's what you mean."

"It isn't. A tigress can have passions—or, as you say, a crocodile. It's her sensibilities I'm wondering about—and whether she could know the other kind of love, the kind that isn't so—so zoological. What do you think?"

But Benvenuto had no time to tell her what he thought, for as the dance ended they stopped opposite a doorway where Mr. and Mrs. Pindlebury were standing, and were greeted by them.

"Been waiting for you," announced Mr. Pindlebury, shortly. "Saw you with the Stokes. Didn't butt in. Infernal blackguard. Sorry if he's a friend of yours. Come and have a drink."

Ann was already walking off, her arm linked in Mrs. Pindlebury's, and Benvenuto, inwardly cursing this board ship life that resembled a railway journey on which one changed at every station, followed with Mr. Pindlebury.

CHAPTER XII
ROMEO AND JULIET

SEATED IN A quiet corner of the lounge, Mr. Pindlebury gave an order to the steward, and then addressed himself to Ann.

"I suppose I'm old-fashioned, my dear," he said, "but I don't like to see you dancing with that fellah Stoke. Your father wouldn't have liked it. The man's a cad. I don't know what the country's coming to. Confound it, sir," he turned to Benvenuto, "one meets him everywhere. Why, I resigned from one of my clubs the other day when I found he'd been made a member. Secretary had the cheek to tell me the man was in the peerage. 'Peerage be damned,' I said."

"I'm afraid," said Benvenuto, "that I was responsible for his meeting Mrs. Stewart. You see, I was talking to Lady Stoke this afternoon, and—"

"Saw you," said Mr. Pindlebury. "Behind a palm tree, but I saw you. Quite a different matter. Damn' good-looking woman. There's always been a place in society for women like her, though perhaps not quite the place they hold to-day. But her husband—by God, sir, I saw him smoke a cigar with a Cockburn 'eighty-six."

"Now, now, Pindlebury," said his wife mildly, picking up a stitch.

"I suppose they're the aristocracy of the future," said Benvenuto. "Great families have been founded by people of Lord Stoke's type; only nowadays instead of conquering with the sword they corner the Stock markets. I was looking the other day at the family portraits in the palace of an English duke—and it was interesting to see the gradual fining down of the features from the original holder of the title, who was, I believe, a blacksmith's son, to the present holder. With each generation the nose lengthened a trifle, the forehead developed, the chin receded, and the bags became more pronounced under the eyes. I wonder what does it—good food and soft beds?"

"Probably marrying into decent stock," snorted Mr. Pindlebury illogically.

Ann laughed. "I suppose," she said, "that if the Stokes produced a son, with her physical beauty and his ruthlessness and intelligence—for he *is* intelligent—the result would be rather startling. Something between a Borgia and a Medici."

"One must try," said Benvenuto, "to avert one's thoughts from a daughter with his beauty and her intelligence."

"Poor little mite," exclaimed Mrs. Pindlebury. "I can't bear to think of it. Is it to be soon, Ann dear? I didn't notice anything—"

Mr. Pindlebury coughed explosively. "Really, Margaret, really! Do pay attention. Pure hypothesis the whole thing. That's the worst of women—never can discuss anything abstract."

"Babies aren't abstract *at all*, Pindlebury, as you'd know if you'd had anything to do with them," said his wife with dignity, as she returned to her knitting.

"Thank God," said Mr. Pindlebury, when his exasperation had subsided, "I was born early enough to see something of the old régime. I'm sorry for you young people—you know nothing about normal life. London before the war was a place worth living in, a decent, mannerly place, sir, where Society stood for something. You wouldn't have found a bounder like the fellah Stoke allowed across a decent doorway. Class meant something in those days—it's ceased to exist to-day—it's been killed by Class-Consciousness. It's a terrible state of things, sir, terrible!" He drank some brandy and shook his head.

"I never go near the town nowadays, can't stand seeing it full of bounders dressed as gentlemen, and gentlemen dressed as bounders. And women! By God, sir, it's—it's frightening. The streets are full of them, morning, noon and night. Twenty years ago no respectable woman was seen in the West End after dark—they had something better to do than idling about in omnibuses and drinking in bars. Monstrous! And what do they get out of it? Nothing, sir—nothing, I tell you. They're thin, neurotic and discontented. They've let us down, sir. They're responsible for all the trouble to-day."

"What makes you think that?" inquired Benvenuto.

"It's obvious! The British workman finds he's got to provide his wife with silk stockings and take her to the moving pictures every night, and what's the result? Before he knows where he is, he's singing the Red Flag and demanding more pay and shorter hours, talking about the Rights of the Working Classes, and the Brotherhood of Man. Brotherhood my foot, sir. It's the Sisterhood of Women at the bottom of it."

"And were you so satisfied," inquired Ann, "with the results of your man-made world? Wasn't the war proof enough that the old system was a failure?"

Mr. Pindlebury looked round at her with a start; he had forgotten her presence.

"Nothing to do with it," he retorted. "There have always been wars, there always will be. Only there'll be twice as many as before, now that women have started screaming at each other across the frontiers."

"Surely," said Benvenuto, "it wasn't so much that the old system was a failure as that we grew out of it. It was doomed to come to an end before the war happened. The war merely hurried things up, sent them all up in smoke. The social system is under-going a period of forced growth, and growth is a painful affair."

Mr. Pindlebury shook his head vigorously. "Nonsense, sir. 'Tisn't growth, it's rot we're suffering from. I tell you human beings knew what they were about when they fell into separate classes, and invented the conventions. You can't play a game without abiding by the rules. When people start to cheat it's the beginning of the end. Look at America—a country with even less respect for law and order and the conventions than we have ourselves. What's the result? Chaos, sir;

bootleggers, gangsters and kidnappers. Respectable citizens being shot down in the street. Battle, murder and sudden death. Call that progress?"

"Yes," said Ann. "It's a sign of progress, or of vitality at least. I can't see much difference between the gangsters of America, and the men who went out and conquered half the world for England, except that they work on a smaller scale. We've got into a habit of calling *them* heroes and Empire builders, but they were mostly pirates and brigands really. The point is, that they all have the same quality—Frances Drake or Al Capone. The quality of personal courage. They are real people who go for what they want without counting the cost. That's why they're dangerous. They seem to be the only people who *have* got courage. It's easy to sit in an arm-chair and criticize. Don't you realize the old laws are no good? People have outgrown them, they're cunning, they can outwit them. Until we've built up some new ones to fit our new world, we have to act alone, on our own responsibility, according to our lights—unless we want to sit back and be ruled by people who are dead and buried."

She paused, a little breathless, then went on in a lower tone:

"Perhaps we've grown out of universal codes. You admit the old laws can't deal with the new criminals. Perhaps we've come to a stage when everyone must act for himself, right his own wrongs, deal out his own vengeance. It's every man for himself now. Perhaps we'll make a better job of it!" Ann finished her outburst with a laugh that was strange and sharp, and that broke in the middle.

Mr. Pindlebury gazed at her in alarm. "God bless my soul, Ann—whoever's been putting these ideas into your head? You're—you're hysterical, my dear; you don't know what you're talking about. Every man for himself, eh? It's every woman you mean, isn't it now? Mrs. Pankhurst all over again. Dear, dear! I wish your father were alive. You're overwrought, you know—very natural, of course. What you want is a long holiday and a change of scene—er—isn't it, Margaret?"

"Nonsense, Pindlebury," said his wife calmly. "Ann is a very clever girl. And if she does ride about in buses, what does it matter? There is nothing immodest about a bus, and the conductors are most courteous. You are getting old-fashioned, Pindlebury—yes, you are!" Mrs. Pindlebury's face was pink as her knitting-wool as she looked defiantly at her husband. He for his part looked round the table in pained amazement, and leant back in his chair, mopping his brow with his handkerchief.

"What an optimist you are," said Benvenuto to Ann.

"*I!*" She stared at him. "I should love to know why you think so."

"You must have a superb faith in human nature if you think you can run an army without a General, which is what your philosophy amounts to, doesn't it? The Russians had the same idea about their ships, you know; they thought it would be anti-Soviet to have officers, so they arranged that everyone should have equal responsibility. It worked all right till they ran into bad weather."

Ann frowned. "I haven't a philosophy. I haven't any theories about how life ought to be run. I haven't any convictions about the future. The only thing I have got to hold on to at all is a kind of faith—a certainty—a conviction if you like—about how I must act myself. Whether my actions are in accordance with the law or contrary to it is immaterial to me. The old ways don't seem to me to have produced anything very good. I can't respect them. I haven't got enough intelligence or vision to construct anything better. But at least I know what *I* must do. If I lost that certainty—then—I would be lost indeed." Her voice trailed off into almost a whisper. She was not talking to him, Benvenuto thought. She was talking to herself.

Mr. Pindlebury got to his feet abruptly. "Margaret, it's time you were in bed. You too, Ann." He patted her rather nervously on the shoulder; he still looked as if he had had a bit of a shock, but his air of authority was gradually returning to him.

"Get some flesh on your bones, girl, and some colour back in your cheeks, and you'll find the problems of the universe will settle themselves without your bothering your pretty head about them. Take my word for it. Come along, Margaret."

He walked to the door with Benvenuto. "We must have a talk some time," he said. "Can't talk with women about. Besides, I want to hear how your latest case is getting along. Good night."

As the Pindleburys left them, Ann and Benvenuto went out on deck. She was smiling faintly as she walked beside him.

"Probably you've no idea," she said, "what a relief it is to find you don't mind any more what people think of you."

"Not a very clear idea," said Benvenuto. "It is generally supposed that one has to attain either an advanced stage of philosophy or—one's death-bed—before one can say that with conviction. What made you say it?"

"I suppose I was boasting," she said. "I was really thinking of Samuel Pindlebury, and of the agony I used to suffer when I was growing up, on account of his attitude to female mentality. The worst of it is that when a man believes or expects a woman to be stupid, she automatically becomes stupid, or at least ceases to be able to express herself in words. And the more dumb she becomes the more she feels a kind of resentful rage against him, and all his kind."

Benvenuto ran both hands through his hair.

"What terrifying creatures women are. I shall feel like a bull in a china shop every time I speak to one in future."

"You needn't," said Ann. "You see, you're one of the few men who talk to women as though they were part of the human race, and not a rather unaccountable phenomena. Haven't you ever noticed how the Press persists, even to-day, in thinking the presence of 'a number of women' at a famous trial or a street accident is remarkable? It never seems to me particularly strange considering what a lot more women than men there are in the world. I suppose even journalists will get over their surprise one day."

"You mustn't confuse ordinary men with journalists," said Benvenuto.

"Perhaps," said Ann, "they are extraordinary men, with a knack of understanding just what constitutes excitement. I suppose it would be much more exciting for men if women *were* rare and mysterious and unexpected creatures. Now that we've got bored with keeping up the illusion, journalists try to do it for us."

"The trouble is," said Benvenuto, "that you *are* rare and mysterious and unexpected. I am still shattered by what you told me about your reaction to the patronizing male, who probably never meant to be patronizing at all. Every time I speak to a pink-cheeked débutante, I shall be watching my step to make sure I don't arouse a torrent of implacable wrath. You're more mysterious than darkest Africa, all of you."

Ann shook her head. "We are pathetically simple. I feel like a traitor to my sex in telling you how simple we are. We have got minds; and they even resemble your minds—perhaps as much as, and no more, than our bodies resemble your bodies. You'll admit that until quite lately it never occurred to men to look further than our bodies. Even when they did it wasn't the result of unprompted curiosity—it was because we got a bit bored with our bodies and started to draw your attention to our minds. We got dreadfully bored, as soon as our energy stopped being used up with breeding and cooking. So we fished our minds out and furbished them up and preened them."

"And then?" said Benvenuto.

"Then—we displayed them before you. And it was rather a failure because we were dreadfully self-conscious. We still are." Ann sighed. "It's all very exhausting; the *only* way for an average woman to make friends with an average man is through sex appeal."

"Are you suggesting," said Benvenuto, "that it is a blind search for abstract friendship on the part of the female which fills the divorce courts?"

"Certainly!" For the moment Ann's face was cleared of shadow as she laughed at him. "Most women are frightfully hungry for the companionship and friendship of men. Our minds want germinating before they can flourish. And we know by experience that as soon as a man is in love with us, our lack of confidence melts like snow—the barriers are down, the doors are opened, and we have long delicious hours of talk which, if we're clever, can make the foundation of friendship that will last long after the sex business has faded out. If only—"

"I've been looking for you, Ann. I feel there are one or two things we ought to discuss if Mr.—er—Brown will excuse me."

Morton-Blount's slightly portentous tone was markedly rude to Benvenuto, as he came up beside them and peered short-sightedly at Ann. She, after looking at him in a dazed fashion, seemed to draw the familiar shadow across her face and slip back, in an instant, to the dark and troubled world she inhabited.

"Of course," she said nervously, "I had forgotten." She moved away, then turned to Benvenuto. "I'm afraid I must have been making after-dinner speeches," she said. "I'm sorry." She smiled rather drearily and walked off, Morton-Blount beside her.

Benvenuto swore softly. There were many things he had meant to say to her. He felt curiously at a disadvantage with Ann; when she was with him his instinct was to subdue himself to the condition of a receiving set, to win her confidence, to give her an outlet, a safety valve for the dark tangle that existed, he felt, in her mind. He told himself that he had in part succeeded, for though she had not shown him the substance of the shadow which hung over her, at least she had opened some aspects of her mind to him, and had found, he thought, a kind of temporary relief and forgetfulness in doing so. Yet each time when she left him, he had a distressing conviction that for every pace she had taken towards him just so far had she withdrawn again into her secret self, and that he would have to start all over again from the beginning.

He walked gloomily along the deck, his head down, and cannoned into someone who appeared suddenly round a corner, He looked up with an apology on his lips, then stared in surprise at the retreating figure. It was Lord Stoke, apparently in a hurry, and certainly in a bad temper judging by the fleeting glance Benvenuto had caught of his scowling face. Why were all the passengers in this ship so full of temperament, he wondered? Was it perhaps that their livers were upset by the first few days at sea? Even the mild and placid Mrs. Pindlebury had defied her husband in a manner that was, he felt sure, uncustomary.

He decided to go forward and seek solitude on the prow of the ship; and leaving behind him the lights of the promenade deck, he ran down the companion-way and crossed the well-deck. In the half-darkness he found an iron stairway and climbed it. At the top a fresh breeze whipped his face, and he picked his way forward until he could lean over the prow with nothing ahead of him but the curling water and the starlit sky. He drew in deep draughts of the cold salt air and felt himself grow calm. Here in the darkness under the powdered sky the concentrated and restless life of the ship seemed to dwindle in importance. Gradually as he stood alone in the dark peace of the ocean night he became detached and impersonal, so that the crowded men and women behind him became as painted players on a mimic stage, reciting with exaggerated gesture their prejudices and beliefs, their puny loves and hates. If Ann were here beside him, he thought, there would be no problem—her troubles would slide away and leave her sane and free.

What was that sound which caught his ear in a lull in the breeze? He looked round, and there, not six feet away on the further side of a windlass stood two people, locked in each other's arms. As his eyes rested on them their faces became disentangled, and he recognized against the star-lit sky the noble and familiar profile of Rutland King, bent at its familiar screen angle over the raised face of a girl. It was impossible to feel intrusive; for the sum of two and fourpence one could watch this same scene being enacted at the nearest picture palace. All the same, thought Benvenuto, I wish they'd go away. He was about to edge off when Lady Stoke's voice cut through the silence.

"Suppose anyone should see us?" she said.

"'I have night's cloak to hide me from their eyes,'" announced her companion in ringing tones.

"'And but thou love me, let them find me here,

My life were better ended by their hate,

Than death prorogued, waiting of thy love.'"

Lady Stoke sighed. "How beautifully you do put it, Rutland. As I always have said, you ought to write your own scenarios."

Benvenuto turned and crept silently away.

THE THIRD DAY

CHAPTER XIII
WHY—?

"GOOD MORNING," said Benvenuto. "Isn't this grand?"

Ann, leaning over the ship's rail, looked up from the dancing water and smiled at him.

"It's so grand," she said, "that it seems almost superfluous to see any more fine mornings for the rest of one's life."

"Which remark simply goes to show," said Benvenuto, "that you're completely under the spell of the *Atalanta*."

"I don't see what the *Atalanta's* got to do with it."

"That's part of the spell," said Benvenuto darkly. "Let me explain."

They turned and walked along the empty deck; they were the first passengers to leave their cabins on the morning of the third day.

"Haven't you ever noticed," he went on, "that whenever you spend a few days on board ship, your ordinary conception of Time goes all to pieces? To begin with, the days of the week lose their personalities; Monday ceases to be real and earnest, a day without a sense of humour as it is on land; Thursday sheds its especial languorous grace; even Sunday morning loses its potency. And having once got rid of this convention by which we've agreed to divide life up—the rest is easy. Take board-ship friendships—even among the English who regard Time with almost religious respect, they're proverbial—they spring up and blossom on a short ocean passage between people who normally, upon dry land, would take weeks, months, even years to arrive at the same stage of intimacy."

"But *do* they achieve friendship?" said Ann. "I'm not at all sure that board-ship acquaintance lasts further than the landing-stage."

"And why? Merely because Time has resumed his sway, and your ocean companion, as soon as he sets foot on land, becomes self-conscious and distrustful of the indecent haste with which he has confessed his favourite colour and his views on the immortality of the soul. And of course up to a point he's right. Having invented an intricate convention of time which has been carried to such an extent that a cocktail or a marriage service is legal at one hour and illegal the next, naturally we have become unfitted to live without it. We have to spread the process of making friends over a long period of time before we can feel sure about them. Personally I think that's a—a pity. (I almost said a waste of time.) Sympathy and hatred, cold, excitement, depression, happiness and hunger, seem to me to divide up time much better than a clock or a calendar. And talking of hunger—shall we—?"

"Come and have breakfast with me," said Ann, turning down the companion-way.

"I think I always live by board-ship time," she went on later, looking at him across the silver and china of the break-fast table. "It's never interested me very much to wonder how *long* I shall live, but merely how *much*, if you see what I mean. Most of the things that are any good happen in a flash—or at least our consciousness of them does. I grew up in the war when things weren't measured by permanence."

Benvenuto nodded. "You were lucky in some ways. People like myself who were in the war had grown up peace-conscious, so that when things got a bit impermanent we became hysterical about Time. I remember trying to cram an enormous number of experiences into every leave—in case the opportunity didn't occur again—and the result was unsatisfactory because one wasn't acclimatized to living in and for the minute. But you, I take it, are."

Ann nodded as she stirred her coffee. "I suppose I've never got properly adjusted to peace. It seemed extremely odd when it happened, I remember. Going to bed with no search-lights in the sky, or shrapnel in the pear trees. Realizing that one's remaining brothers and cousins and friends were permanent features of one's life instead of people who passed through it. But being war-conscious has its disadvantages, you know." She smiled faintly. "One has had to do without religion and codes of morals, and the acceptance of convention and all the other comforts that our parents enjoyed. I believe they, having acquired them all in early life, managed to adjust them to war conditions. Look at the Pindleburys! But I arrived at the wrong moment for acquiring them. I simply couldn't make them fit. I've often thought I'd like to try them out, but I can't."

"You mean you haven't discovered the world to be a place run according to some logical plan under the direction of a purposeful president?"

"I admit I haven't. Life seems to me to be a game for which one has to invent the rules as one goes along. The moment you start blindly accepting other people's rules for your own use, you begin to die."

"Do you realize you're consigning at least nine-tenths of your fellow creatures to their graves?" inquired Benvenuto.

"But don't you think they *are* dead, most of them?" Ann looked at him queerly. "To have eyes that don't see and ears that don't hear seems to me very death-like. Look at the people in this ship—listen to them talking. They take care to preserve life without even being curious about it. I don't think it's worth preserving if the cost is denying an experience or a—a job of work. None of the people who've done things have valued existence for its own sake."

Benvenuto laughed. "You don't like a man who feels his own pulse. Well, I agree with you. On the other hand recklessness for its own sake can cheat you out of life just as surely as prudence."

Ann, staring down at the table cloth, seemed when she spoke to be talking to herself.

"It's not recklessness," she murmured. "It's just—being able to see your own road. I never made anything of my life— But at least I wasn't asleep all the time."

At the moment she might just as well be asleep, or in a trance, thought Benvenuto, watching her abstracted face. She had slipped away again into her secret brooding solitude. Discomfort crept over him, discomfort that grew and changed to fear. For a moment as he watched her, his mind was stilled with a nameless foreboding, strange and yet familiar. Life was playing a trick with him, repeating itself in a dark and familiar rhythm. It was as though, entering a strange country for the first time in his life, he knew and recognized its form and vegetation, knew what he would see round the next corner, heard words before they were spoken, the strain of music before it was played. He had slipped out of the formal procession of events and hovered in space, a creature of dreams, or, more fearfully, a creature chained to a life of endless repetitions—

With a sharp effort he pulled himself together and knew, in a flash of relief, where he had lived through those moments before. It was in no dream world, no forgotten existence; it was but two nights before when, looking across the water with Ann, he had felt her mind slip away from him, into some world where he had no place. And then she had been brought back to reality by something outside both their lives—by a drowning woman.

He bent across the table, closer to her pale face.

"Why do you want to murder Lord Stoke?" he said.

CHAPTER XIV
BEFORE THE FACT

HE WISHED she would stop laughing. It made him feel guilty, as though he had by accident released a rushing stream, and had no power to stop its course. Was she laughing at him, at herself, at the absurdity of the world in general? Her laughter ran on and on, rippling through her body, shaking her. It was worse than the few moments of frozen silence which had preceded it. Suddenly with a little gasp she stopped.

"If you are a psycho-analyst," she said, "how disappointed you must be that I only laughed. It's as though you'd said 'strawberry' in the hope that I'd reply 'blood,' and then I'd only said 'cream.' I'm *so* sorry. But it must be a good game. Do you play it much?"

Benvenuto took out his cigarette case and passed it to her. Her fingers, as she shielded the flame of his match from draught, were steady.

"All the same," he said, "I think it's a pity if you won't tell me why you want to murder Lord Stoke. After all, I might agree with you."

She blew out a puff of smoke and smiled at him. "So we play a second round? I wish I were better at your game. That's the worst of ship sports. One only begins to acquire the technique on the last day of the voyage, and if one's an exhibitionist as I am, it's rather trying. I do hate doing things badly. Let *me* ask *you* a question now. Where was it you acquired the habit of eating babies' toes in your soup?"

"That was in Upper Bolivia," said Benvenuto. "You interest me extraordinarily, you know," he went on. "Mr. Gowling, now, appears to me to have quite an adequate reason for desiring the death of Lord Stoke. Also he's the type who would delight in revenge so long as it entailed no personal risk. But why *you* should wish to extinguish the spark of life in that gross and unattractive body is another story, and an intriguing one. Won't you tell it me?"

Her smile was rather chilly and aloof, now.

"I don't wish to seem stupid," she said, "but I must confess I'm rather at sea. You've apparently been discussing me with Mr. Gowling; the result makes me wonder if he's gone out of his mind or—forgive me—if you have."

"You do him an injustice," said Benvenuto. "He stoutly though rather inartistically denied that you have any part in the murder plot. It was you, yourself, if you'll forgive me, who convinced me of your intentions."

For the first time since he had known her he saw the blood creep into Ann's face, so that her pale skin seemed as though it reflected a pink light. Her eyes were dark now, burning, flashing at him. She was biting her lips, speechless. At last, "If your convictions were less outrageous, less intolerable—I should find it easier to realize what you mean. Are you really—seriously—trying to tell me I'm a—murderess?"

"Not at all," said Benvenuto. "Evidently I've expressed it wrongly. I meant that I realize you *want* to kill someone—and I doubt if there's anyone alive who hasn't had the instinct to murder at some time or other in their lives. That's what makes murderers so difficult to catch—there is no criminal type. Have you ever realized the enormous number of unsuspected murderers there are whose victims either disappear or lie comfortably under neat tomb-stones, their deaths the supposed result of illness or accident?"

"I'm afraid I haven't," said Ann, "and I suggest your view of humanity is slightly warped. In any case I should be glad if you would leave me out of your gallery of criminals and pick on some other passenger in this ship for your extraordinary accusations. Preferably a man. Good-bye."

"Don't go," said Benvenuto. "Please sit down." He was surprised, as he stood facing her, to find he was trembling.

"Do sit down for God's sake! We've said too much for you to leave me like this. Listen—I'll send a note to Morton-Blount's cabin, asking him to come here. When he comes, if he doesn't say—what I believe he will say—I'll spend the rest of the voyage apologizing to you. You must do this for me. Please sit down."

And Ann sat down. Still and pale, she sat opposite to him while he scribbled a note and sent it by a hurrying steward.

Please God, the fellow's up and dressed, he thought as he looked at Ann across the table.

For her part she took not the slightest notice of him, and stared out of the porthole, a frozen figure of wrath.

How long would she stay there? Benvenuto considered rapidly; if his conviction was right her stillness concealed nerves stretched to breaking point—nerves which might snap at any moment and send her flying from the room, running into Heaven knew what desperate and fatal action. If he were wrong—here his mind shied, but he forced himself to the consideration—why then, her stillness meant she was facing as philosophically as possible the problem of sharing her breakfast table with a lunatic. Benvenuto almost groaned aloud as the minutes slipped by, minutes during which the tinkle of spoons and cups, voices and laughter, and the hurrying feet of stewards formed an unreal accompaniment to his and Ann's frozen silence. If Morton-Blount is asleep, he thought; if he takes no notice of the message; if—

But Morton-Blount was not asleep; he had entered the room and was coming towards them. His tie was a little askew as though he had hurried with his dressing, but otherwise he looked his normal self with his falling lock of hair, his glasses, and the books under his arm. He blinked amiably as he sat down and seemed a little sleepy.

"Good morning," he said, "I got your message. I—"

"Good morning, Blount," said Benvenuto. "Why do you want to murder Lord Stoke?"

Ann flashed round to him, her fingers gripping his arm. But Morton-Blount took no notice of her. His eyes behind his thick glasses were alight with fervour as he leant towards Benvenuto.

"Because the Five Year Plan is doomed to failure unless we do," he said.

CHAPTER XV
'FOOLS THAT WISH TO DIE'

As a brick thrown into a still pool breaks the silver surface and makes ripples which, fading, leave behind them water streaked and clouded by the muddy depths below—so Morton-Blount's admission spread a circle of disturbance which slowly settled again into a false calm. But the mud had stirred, the hidden depths had shown on the surface, and each of the three people at the table waited for another to speak first.

Benvenuto's thoughts raced. He was right, but he found no sense of triumph in his own cleverness. He must be cleverer still now, and watch each step, each word. At this moment he was further than ever, he thought, from gaining Ann's confidence. She had shrunk into herself, a strange, bitter half-smile on her lips, her large eyes fixed on him defiantly. Morton-Blount sat forward, his mouth open, his face unnaturally red, looking like a boy who has misbehaved at a party.

"Tea or coffee, sir?"

Morton-Blount jumped as if he had been stung, stammered an order for coffee and nothing to eat, and looked again at Benvenuto.

"I wonder," said Benvenuto, choosing his words and speaking slowly, "whether you will both agree with me when I say that I have now become a factor in your private plans. A nuisance, naturally; perhaps an obstacle; perhaps on the other hand a help. Will you treat me frankly, as I want to treat you; tell me the whole story, and let me then decide what I'm going to do?"

"No," said Ann swiftly, "do what you like." She leant forward. "Or better still, do nothing. You are clever. Aren't you clever enough to forget all about us?"

"No," said Benvenuto. "I'm not clever enough for that."

"Let me explain—" began Morton-Blount, but Ann again laid her hand upon his arm and spoke.

"Why should we explain? Don't you see that it can do no good? Is it likely that Mr. Brown, if we talked to him for months, would believe what we believe, or feel as we feel? You have done enough harm already, Roger. Do you want the whole ship to know our affairs, which are private—*private*. What good could it do us, what good could it do Mr. Brown, if he knew more than he does now?"

"Well, really, Ann, I think you're quite wrong," replied Morton-Blount. "I *would* like to tell everyone on the ship. I'd like to make a speech to all the sailors and stewards, the workers, the Comrades, to tell them of this tremendous thing which must be saved for them—must be used for their good, for the good of Humanity, instead of being used as another weapon against them, to beat them down, enslave them. They have a Right to know. When I think of all these people sitting here in complacent ease—" his hand swept round the dining-saloon—"it makes me want to rise up and show them the truth. What do they know of the lives of the men who serve them—the underpaid and overworked, the poor devils of stokers sweating blood down in the furnaces—"

"Not the stokers," said Benvenuto sharply.

Arrested in full flight Morton-Blount looked at him impatiently.

"Why not?" he inquired.

"Well, there aren't any stokers in an oil-driven ship," said Benvenuto.

But Morton-Blount waved the fact aside. Still trembling with emotion, his short-sighted eyes looked across the saloon—to a vision of Proletarian agony. Absent-mindedly he gulped at his hot coffee.

Benvenuto smoked thoughtfully. Was it possible that what lay behind Ann's eyes was the fanaticism of social revolution, the crusade of the workers; the Hot Gospel of Liberty, Equality and Fraternity spread by the bomb and the hidden assassin? He thought not. Morton-Blount was easy enough to draw out; he was only too eager to justify himself. But Ann? Why should she want to murder Lord Stoke? And why, if it came to that, should Morton-Blount? The secret of the fertilizer was his Holy Grail, his panacea for the world's wrongs; surely if he had that to hand over to the Workers, the death of its present owner was not necessary or even excusable, except from the point of view that all Capitalists should be bumped off on principle.

"I am going to put my cards on the table," said Benvenuto suddenly, "and trust that you will do the same. I know Mr. Gowling's story, though I am not, at the moment, free to tell you how I know it. Up to a point I sympathize with him, and I understand your attitude also, Mr. Morton-Blount. But tell me this: are you going about this affair in the best way? Are not your methods a little crude? Will they not possibly miss their target and recoil upon yourselves? I speak, if you like, as an amateur of crime, as one who hates to see a job bungled."

"We owe you no sort of an apology for our lives or our convictions," said Ann coldly, "and our actions are our own affair. Our plans are laid, and frankly, we neither need a confederate nor particularly fear an enemy. You force me to speak plainly."

She spoke with the casual insolence of an aristocrat who rebukes an impertinence, but Benvenuto told himself that he was not deceived by the arrogance of her answer. For the moment her ruling purpose was forgotten and—he realized it with a rising heart—her efforts were directed towards one object, to keeping him from the gulf towards which she, indifferently, was rushing.

He smiled at her in full understanding, and she lowered her eyes as if asking herself whether he could have understood.

"Mrs. Stewart," he said, "I am not wanted. But I am here. And I intend to remain. If you reject me now as a friend, you force me into the position of a powerful enemy. I can have you and Morton-Blount locked up in ten minutes—and I will. You ask me why, and I say that to me at this moment, knowing only what I do, you are childish and dangerous people, playing with fire. I say that because I know so little—because unless I know more, my only course of action is to prevent you hurting both yourselves and others. Yet—I have an idea that I am—I might be—on your side of the fence; I might be able to help you to attain what you want. Prove to me that you know what you are doing—that you are reasoning creatures with a sane object in view. Why should you not give me your reasons and motives? Are you ashamed of them? I don't believe it. I believe that you have the purest and best motives for what you intend to do. But—you are forcing me into the position either of betraying you or becoming accessory to a fact of which I am ignorant. Is that fair? Why not trust me—and give me a chance, at least, of helping you?"

"We do not need help," said Ann. "And you are horribly wrong. I am not a Joan of Arc longing to die in a good cause. My motives are not pure. My feelings would mean nothing to you. Leave us to ourselves, to live or die as we like. Cannot we die if we wish to? Can't you see that there are some things so intimate and personal that you can't invade them? You have no right to ask me—no right, I tell you."

"Communism and artificial manure seem impersonal enough," murmured Benvenuto, glancing round at Morton-Blount.

He regretted it as soon as he had spoken, for Ann rose abruptly to her feet and went towards the door.

He must not let her go; now he was sure that she was capable of any dangerous folly; and that to lose sight of her before he knew more, before he had come to some understanding with her, was madness and death.

Leaving Morton-Blount, he pursued Ann up the staircase and on to the deck, where the tang of salt air touched his face like a chill and reassuring breath of sanity. She was conscious of his pursuit and did not look round. Benvenuto followed, side-stepping to avoid promenading passengers who walked briskly, wrapped in coats and furs. Someone, probably Pindlebury, put a hand on his arm, but he shook himself free without a word, and followed her.

She stopped and leant over the rail, and he stood in a doorway, watching her. She looked out to sea, where a stocky tramp steamer, her blunt nose cutting through the green waves and her smoke blown like a grey plume from her funnel, stolidly attempted her distant port.

Ann's hair, too, blew out as she stood there, letting herself for a moment be battered by the wind, passive and motionless; waiting, it seemed, for a decision to come to her, rather than bracing herself to take it.

And as they stood there, waiting, a new sound came through the air; a throb, faint but insistent, which gradually swelled to a strong harsh pulsation. People rushed to the ship's side, waved their hats, their handkerchiefs, cheered, pointed upwards in unison. Far above them in a blue circle in the clouds an aeroplane was passing over their heads, overtaking the ship, going swiftly towards the west on its fragile and lonely wings, crossing the Atlantic to New York.

Ann stared alter it as it passed, and to Benvenuto it seemed that a decision had come to her; for she turned quickly from the rail, slipped between the people whose eyes were still following the disappearing plane, and walked rapidly away.

Benvenuto, hurrying after her, mounted a companion-way and saw her enter a corridor and disappear into a cabin. It was, he noticed, the next cabin to those occupied by Morton-Blount and Gowling. He hesitated at the entrance of the corridor, his eyes upon her door. Absent-mindedly he lit a cigarette, puffed at it, threw it away. Then he walked quickly to the door and knocked.

There was silence. Then her voice, low and startled, called "Come in."

As he closed the door she was standing facing him, in front of her wardrobe, her hands behind her back. Her face was hard and pale as she stared at him.

He crossed over to where she stood, and drew both her hands from behind her back. He was smiling at her as he took a gun from her suddenly limp fingers.

"You're not very good at this sort of thing, you know," he said. "I could see this deadly weapon reflected in the mirror as I came in." He opened the breech, knocked the charge out into his hand and slipped the small revolver into his pocket. He looked at her, expecting—he knew not what; fury, perhaps, or tears.

But she was perfectly composed. She faced him easily, her head held high, her hands dropped to her sides, her body poised in a slender line of arrogant and unconscious beauty.

Sunlight streamed through the porthole, half blinding him, outlining Ann's figure so that she seemed an unreal two-dimensional creature. But he could see her eyes, the lids drooping half over them; dark eyes that watched him steadily, that seemed half sensuous, half defiant, unconquerable.

"Will you please go—" she said at last.

Benvenuto turned and walked slowly away. It was war—and the first victory was to Ann.

CHAPTER XVI
WATCH DOG

BENVENUTO went down the stairs slowly, thinking. And his thoughts were far from pleasant. Was he afraid of this woman, he asked himself disagreeably, that he crept away, dumbly, when she told him to go? He knew that he was hideously afraid of what she might do, what her mad resolve might lead her to.

He fingered the gun in his pocket, knowing that although its loss might delay her it could not finally deter her.

Ann, this time, had been too strong for him, but the morning had not been entirely wasted, he told himself. He must attack the three-linked chain at a weaker place, speak to Morton-Blount or Gowling alone.

Which should it be?

He looked into the dining-room and found it deserted—Morton-Blount had gone and stewards were laying the tables for lunch. Trying to find anyone on board ship was like chasing a mosquito in the dark, thought Benvenuto. Better to sit down and wait until they reappeared, which everyone seemed to do sooner or later.

He went into the smoking-room and looked round. Seated in a corner was Mr. Gowling, leaning back smoking a cigar, and surveying the rest of the passengers with an air of Napoleonic superiority. Benvenuto, unasked, took the opposite chair and nodded to him.

"Feeling better this morning, Mr. Gowling?"

"Quite orlright, thanks," replied the other, eyeing him in a somewhat hostile manner.

"And how," asked Benvenuto, "is your affair getting on?"

Mr. Gowling laughed in what he apparently considered a rather cynical fashion, then laughed again as if genuinely amused.

"Pullin' yer leg the 'ole time," he said, leaning confidentially across the table, "just to see 'ow much you'd swaller. I've always been a bit of a humorist."

He laughed again, then winked and added:

"It comes of not mindin' yer own business. Mind yer own business and yer won't go getting told fairy stories, like mine was, see?"

"I congratulate you," said Benvenuto.

"Granted," said Mr. Gowling, pleased with this tribute.

"I mean I congratulate you on the success of your new method of dealing with Lord Stoke," said Benvenuto at a venture.

The effect of this random shot was instantaneous. Mr. Gowling's mouth dropped open, and he looked fishily at Benvenuto, who thought it worth while to make sure of his ground by adding:

"Blackmail is useful sometimes, isn't it, Mr. Gowling?"

But Mr. Gowling, limply, had gone.

Benvenuto laughed. He was making slow progress, but one by one the irregular unmeaning shapes of his jig-saw puzzle were falling into place, and from the corner he had completed he seemed to see a blurred and misty vision of the whole.

He rose abruptly, and went out to look for Morton-Blount.

After ten minutes' search he came upon him sitting on a settee in the lounge. Somewhat to his surprise Morton-Blount rose when he saw him, and greeted him effusively.

"Well met," he said in his high-pitched and rather over-cultivated voice. "How singularly difficult it is to find anyone whom one wishes to find in this ship. I have been making an exhaustive search for you. Won't you sit down?"

He was smiling with unaccustomed cordiality but seemed extremely nervous. Benvenuto sat down beside him upon the opulently comfortable settee, and leaning back in a bed of cushions waited for him to continue.

Morton-Blount coughed and began to fidget with a paper-knife with which he had been cutting the pages of a book.

"To revert to our conversation at breakfast," he said at last, "you may remember that we were discussing a certain plan of action which had been determined on by Mrs. Stewart, Mr. Gowling and myself. I now feel I ought to tell you that there is no likelihood—or possibility—of anything of the kind happening. I have been talking with Ann—"

Benvenuto could have told him that.

"And we realize that this Plan of ours—formulated in a moment of enthusiasm—is now—er—abortive."

"Because of me?" inquired Benvenuto politely.

"Exactly."

"You've given up the idea of—eliminating—Lord Stoke?"

"Again—exactly."

"Well," said Benvenuto, "I think you're extremely wise."

Morton-Blount smiled perfunctorily and made an effort to rise from his cushioned seat, but Benvenuto's hand restrained him.

"A moment, if you don't mind. You see, I have only got your word for your intentions, and for all I know you might change your mind again. Now, let's get this clear. I gather that what you really want is the formula for this fertilizer of Gowling's, and if you had that you would be satisfied?"

Morton-Blount removed his glasses and looked at them.

"Yes—that is—I don't see the slightest chance of this man Stoke parting with the formula; and do you realize he will make the most vile use of it? American Capitalism will control the cheap food supply of the world for its own profit. It will buy armies, it will be master of the world; it will be all-powerful; it will crush Communism and the Soviets." Morton-Blount's voice rose higher and higher as he went on.

"The Brotherhood of Man will be only a dream for perhaps hundreds of years. I can't bear to think of it. But, on the other hand, brother—" he turned to Benvenuto, his weak eyes oddly pathetic without their glasses, "just imagine this vast Power in the hands of Stalin! Imagine Russia powerful, conquering; able at last to impose the superb ideas of Lenin upon the grasping bankers, able to set free the glorious proletariat from their kings and slave-drivers, until the Social Revolution has embraced the globe and every man is a unit in the Industrial State!"

Benvenuto shuddered slightly.

"Neither alternative sounds very peaceful for the next few generations," he said mildly.

"World Revolution—*then* Peace."

"And Mrs. Stewart shares your views?"

"Certainly," replied Morton-Blount, the visionary glow fading from his eyes, and a certain uneasiness taking its place. He polished his spectacles briskly and replaced them on his nose.

"And you both think it better to destroy the owner of this formula rather than allow it to be exploited by the Capitalists?"

Morton-Blount's tone was sulky as he said: "I told you we'd given up that idea."

Benvenuto looked at him speculatively and murmured: "I see." Then: "I'm afraid I've not taken this fertilizer very seriously up till now. I've been, as a matter of fact, rather busy with something else. You think Lord Stoke really *does* possess this extraordinary secret?"

"I am sure of it. I have—er—a source of information other than Mr. Gowling. But I am at a loss to understand how you know of the existence of the formula."

Benvenuto ignored the implied question and got slowly to his feet.

"I'd like to think this over and talk to you later. How about this evening?"

Morton-Blount nodded. "I'd like to convert you to my ideas," he said with missionary fervour, laying his hand shyly upon Benvenuto's arm.

Benvenuto took a gulp of clean salt air as he hurried along the deck. Are zealots always like that, he wondered? Was it the Morton-Blounts of antiquity that had once held Christianity in abeyance for four hundred years? He ran up the steps to the Captain's office.

Sir George Beckworth was seated at his desk talking to one of his officers. He dismissed the officer and motioned Benvenuto to a chair.

"Not a bit of it," he said as Benvenuto apologized. "Come along any time you want me. My ship seems more in need of a squad of police than a commander. Have you any news for me?"

"I'm afraid I haven't come to report progress so much as to ask for assistance." He paused to take a cigarette from the Captain's case.

"Look here, sir, don't think I am trying to be officious or—er—melodramatic, but I want you if you will to put a good man on guard over Lord Stoke for the rest of the day. At, say, half-past ten to-night I'll relieve him myself. I haven't told Lord Stoke that I'm asking you to do this—there's no point in scaring him unnecessarily. But I should feel a good deal more comfortable if you could arrange to have him kept under the eve of a discreet and reliable man who will be on the alert for any kind of an attack."

Sir George Beckworth smoked silently for a few moments.

"Have you any reason, other than the anonymous letter, for asking me to do this?" he said.

"Yes," said Benvenuto.

Again there was silence.

"You shall have your watch dog," said the Captain at last. "I'll see to it at once. I haven't had to do any blind flying for a long time," he added, smiling.

"I'm flying blind myself, sir," said Benvenuto, "so I appreciate your attitude."

The Captain walked with him to the door.

"At the risk of intruding on another man's duties," he said, "I should like to know if you have made any progress in that other affair—Miss Smith."

"I believe," said Benvenuto, "that I have. Yesterday I sent a wireless to a friend of mine in the C.I.D. and when I get his answer—I ought to get it tomorrow—I may be able to report something definite to you. Can we leave it at that for the moment, sir?"

He went off to lunch, feeling profoundly grateful for the unquestioning co-operation of Sir George Beckworth.

CHAPTER XVII
ŒDIPUS COMPLEX

As TRAVELLING companions, thought Benvenuto gratefully, the Pindleburys were perfect. Stretched upon either side of him in deck chairs they were digesting their lunch, and beyond an occasional smiling nod from Mrs. Pindlebury and an interchange of matches with her husband, they had left him undisturbed for almost two hours.

With Ann lying down in her cabin, with Morton-Blount making notes on the margin of a Blue Book in the lounge, with Mr. Gowling courting unpopularity upon the quoits deck, and Lord Stoke under guard, Benvenuto lay in the sun. He smoked, dipped into "Candide" and allowed his thoughts to wander.

The promenade deck was a very pleasant place upon which to do it. From his chair he could watch the blue line of the horizon gently changing places with the ship's rail, watch the sunlight upon water of which the morning placidity was now livened by a slight movement, and watch the promenading passengers who crossed his line of vision and gave to the *Atalanta* something of the air of a fashion parade. The clear afternoon sunlight wasn't particularly kind to the make-up on the faces of the women, make-up that had acquired emphasis, he decided, from life in artificially lit apartments. But they had extraordinary chic, these American women—a kind of vigorous clean-cut smartness.

His eyes wandered back to the Pindleburys. Mr. Pindlebury, in pepper and salt tweeds and a dark grey cap, was examining *Punch* through his monocle, while his wife, her silver hair held in place by a net and the locket on her placid bosom winking in the sun, was counting the stitches on her needles. They might have been sitting on the terrace of their country house, thought Benvenuto; they carried with them the comfortable atmosphere of the Midlands, of low-built manor houses and green fields, of the slow rhythm of country life with its traditions and its quiet ease. They were pleasant reassuring people to be with when half of one's mind ran upon murder and blackmail.

Then he forgot them as he saw a girl walking down the deck. She was almost too appropriately dressed in a nautically inspired confection of blue and white, but he forgave her that as she came nearer. She was perhaps twenty, slender and ravishing, with the sun shining on her pale hair. She was, he realized, the American blonde whose grey eyes had caught and held his own on that first day at lunch. As she passed him her dark lashes fluttered for a moment in his direction and her walk became a shade self-conscious.

Benvenuto absent-mindedly rubbed his nose, and shut his volume of "Candide." But his next action was arrested by Mr. Pindlebury who had risen to his feet and was stretching himself elaborately.

"Deplorable effect on the liver, all this sitting about," he explained, "going to get some exercise. See you later."

"I'll come with you," said Benvenuto. "I'd like a stroll."

But Mr. Pindlebury appeared confused. "No, no, don't you bother. Have a talk with Margaret. As a matter-of-fact I've got some letters to write." And he set off hurriedly down the deck.

Benvenuto, subsiding into his deck chair, found Mrs. Pindlebury was nodding and twinkling at him over her knitting.

"You mustn't take any notice of Pindlebury," she said. "I suppose you think he's very mysterious—but he isn't at all."

She beckoned to him with a long bone needle, and raising her wrinkled and smiling face she whispered in his ear: "It's the Œdipus complex!"

"The Œdipus complex—" echoed Benvenuto faintly.

She had drawn back and was watching him delightedly, rather like a child enjoying the effect of a surprise packet. Then she nodded again and returned to her knitting.

"Yes—that's how it all began. I'll tell you about it, but you mustn't give me away, you know."

"I won't give you away," said Benvenuto.

"No, I know you won't. You understand people. Like dear Doctor Schnitzler. But I'm coming to that."

She settled more comfortably into her chair and clicked her needles busily.

"Pindlebury has been rather ill, you know. At least, not ill exactly, but—*queer*. Moody and quite cross at times. Then he started going for long walks in the London parks late at night. By himself you know. So I got quite worried about him, poor man—such unfortunate things happen, don't they?" She looked brightly round at Benvenuto and went on.

"I knew you'd understand. Well, in the end I persuaded him to come and see a doctor—a psycho-analyst, though of course I didn't tell Pindlebury that. Such a charming man, *so* understanding. He did wonders for the husband of a friend of mine, in fact, *saved* him I always think. We were dreadfully afraid at one time he would lose his circuit. However, dear Pindlebury proved a very difficult case. Unfortunately he took quite a dislike to Dr. Schnitzler—what was it he called him? Dear me—yes—an 'inquisitive bounder'—that was it. You see how difficult it was. Of course it is all part of the symptoms. Pindlebury is *so* full of Resistances."

For a moment Mrs. Pindlebury sighed, then went on.

"So sweet of you to be so understanding. I never talk about this to *anyone*. And you've no idea how tiresome it is—" She looked at him appealingly—"to have to practice subterfuges. There's my tooth-ache. Pindlebury thinks I suffer dreadfully with my teeth because I have to go to London so frequently to see the dentist. I'm so thankful it isn't really a dentist, I never *have* been able to like one, although poor dears, one mustn't be unchristian, and they do have such horrid lives looking into people's mouths. Dear Doctor Schnitzler is so delightful, it is quite a pleasure to go to see him. Not for myself, you know. When poor Pindlebury refused to see him again, of course I had to do what I could. I couldn't let him go on being so queer. You do see that, don't you?"

"I think you must be very fond of your husband," said Benvenuto gently.

"He's everything in the world to me. We never had any children—such a pity, it might have made all the difference—given him an interest. I expect you think Pindlebury is a man of the world with all his talk of fine women and big bosoms and so on—but he isn't, you know. He's dreadfully innocent, quite inexperienced. That's why I'm so worried about him. He had such an unfortunate upbringing—he adored his mother, and his father was so unkind to her, even violent at times. Drank, I believe, poor man. Dr. Schnitzler says it set up a Complex in Pindlebury. Then he had a most unhappy love affair, at least it ended unhappily. I think she was rather common, a shop girl you know, but so sweet and pretty, and she had a little baby and it died, and then she died—at least, I think she did, and poor Pindlebury was really heartbroken, and then he found me. I comforted him and he asked me to marry him, and I did, and—well, I've been comforting him ever since. But men have to have more than comfort, don't they?"

Mrs. Pindlebury was still smiling but she looked a little wistful now.

"I think," said Benvenuto, "that you're unfair to yourself. Mr. Pindlebury adores you."

"So sweet of you to say so," she was all brightness again, and picked up her knitting. "He *is* very fond of me, I know. And I often say to myself, after all perhaps Pindlebury *might* not have been happy with his Fanny even if she had lived. You see he was so *dreadfully* in love with her, and what was it Oscar Wilde said: 'For each man kills the thing he loves—' Poor Mr. Wilde, I often think he knew a great deal about psycho-analysis, though of course it wasn't called that then. There now, I've dropped a stitch."

She bent her head over the pink wool for the light was failing a little. But Benvenuto stared out across the darkening sea, his brain whirling, his hands gripping the rail of his chair, and forgot to condole with her.

Fanny!

Slowly he turned and looked at the woman beside him. She was a sweet and placid figure, from her comfortable well-made shoes to her silver hair. The net which held her hair in place had blown a little askew in the wind, and one small curl had escaped, which gave her a slight air of rakishness. Her kindly face, bent now over a tangle of purl and plain was delicately lined as though even age respected her, and the dimpled hands which flashed her needles were fresh as a girl's. He could see those hands moving among tea cups, arranging flowers—

What was it Ann had said? "For her, the world is a pleasant place, half flower garden, half drawing-room, where people are gentle with each other and kind to animals—"

A man would do much, thought Benvenuto, to keep trouble from that placid head.

Suddenly she looked up at him.

"Oh, dear, I've been boring you dreadfully with my little troubles. You look quite tired. Why don't you run along and find Ann, such a dear girl. I think I'll go to my cabin now—the sea is getting up a little, don't you think? I do hope it isn't going to be rough."

But before she could rise, a steward was bending over her with a tray, on which were two glasses, and a bottle of champagne in an ice bucket.

"I think this is for you, madam," he said.

"Oh, no!" Mrs. Pindlebury shook her head smilingly. "That's for my husband. Just let me look at the label. Yes, that's quite correct. Find out where he is and take it to him."

She turned to Benvenuto.

"That is the Veuve Clicquot 1911. So fortunate they have it on board. It does Pindlebury *so* much good, breaks down his inhibitions, you know. I only *hope* she's a nice girl, and won't laugh at him. Now don't forget," she shook her finger at him, "Pindlebury hasn't the least idea I know anything about it, so you mustn't let him suspect. This is our little conspiracy!"

He helped her to her feet and steadied her for the boat had begun to roll.

"I'll bring your things along for you," he said.

Walking down the deck she held his arm and laughed at herself for her unsteadiness. She had a warm sweet scent of lavender-water and furs.

He put her rugs and magazines in her cabin and held her hand for a moment as he said good-bye.

But he couldn't ask her where Mr. Pindlebury had been two nights before.

CHAPTER XVIII
RECONSTRUCTION

THE *ATALANTA*, like a sea beast playing ponderously at some monstrous sport, rolled heavily upon the water. At one moment she rode high over a wave, at the next a rush of water smacked her triumphantly upon the side, covering her decks with spray, and sending a deep shudder through her vast structure.

Benvenuto, propelling himself with difficulty round the deserted promenade deck, paused upon the leeward side, and going to the rail he leant over it and stared into the threatening dusk.

A dark line showed the demarcation between tumbling grey waters and lowering sky, a sky upon which over-mod-elled clouds, fringed here and there with scudding streaks of white, piled themselves up in angry magnificence. To the west where the ship was heading a sulphuric yellow light showed where the sun was hidden and made a sinister contrast with the inky sky.

Benvenuto, clinging to the rail, felt himself in gloomy sympathy with the day. A sense of fore-boding, caused, he told himself, by the coming storm, had descended on his spirit and he shivered as a gust of wind screamed above his head. He would go and change for dinner, he decided, and take an early cocktail at the bar.

Tramping down the deck and steadying himself from time to time upon the rail as the *Atalanta* lurched, his thoughts revolved persistently round Mr. Pindlebury.

Where had he been two nights before when Miss Smith went to drown in the dark water?

He went over in his mind the events of that evening. Mr. Pindlebury, drinking brandy in the smoking-room, telling him the story of Ann; Mr. Pindlebury in the dance-room, commenting on the modern woman, thwarted in his pursuit of the American blonde; Mr. Pindlebury with his wife. At this point Benvenuto had left them, had gone on deck and met and talked with Miss Smith. He stopped, startled by a sudden memory.

Miss Smith had asked the name of the man to whom he had been talking—and for a moment he had thought she referred to Pindlebury, had even told her his name.

No, he assured himself. It was not Pindlebury who had interested her—it was Gowling. And yet—having got the information she wanted, was it not possible that for some secret reason of her own she had deceived him, had feigned an interest in Gowling?

Frowning, he walked on, and opening a door went into the quiet of a corridor. He wanted to get away from the buffeting wind, to be alone in his cabin and to think.

Suddenly, at the far end of a corridor, he saw Mr. Pindlebury come out of a cabin, and closing the door, start walking towards him. Benvenuto quickened his pace. He would have a talk with him.

But Mr. Pindlebury either did not see him or had other plans, for he turned aside and disappeared.

Benvenuto went to his cabin, pulled out some paper and a pencil and sat down at the table. Could he, by working out the probable dates and times, refute the suspicions that had lodged in his mind while he listened to Mrs. Pindlebury's story?

Samuel Pindlebury, he wrote.

Present age—about sixty.

Miss Smith—age at time of her death, about fifty.

Miss Smith's dead son, probably born about thirty-two years ago.

That would make Mr. Pindlebury twenty-eight at the time of the child's birth, and Miss Smith eighteen. Yes, it was possible that Miss Smith was Fanny.

Troubled and unwilling, he began to construct in his mind the possible chain of events.

Suppose Samuel Pindlebury in his youth had met the common, pretty, and virtuous shop girl, Fanny. He falls in love with her, she with him. He cannot confess the affair to his family for they would disapprove—so there is a secret marriage. Poor Fanny bears him a still-born child—is desperately ill, loses her reason. Samuel Pindlebury, heartbroken and knowing no one to whom he can turn, sees her shut up in an asylum, presumed to be incurably insane. He pays for her keep and tells no one of his marriage.

After a time he meets Margaret, pretty and kind and gentle, and of his own class. She falls in love with him, pleases him, comforts him. Gradually he sees in her the possibility of the happiness that he thought had gone for ever.

What is he to do?

Poor mad Fanny doesn't need him any more. No one else knows of her existence. So he asks Margaret to marry him, and for thirty years they live together in peace and comfort and respectability.

Gradually Mr. Pindlebury allows himself to forget the very existence of Fanny. Provision for her is made through a lawyer, and if he ever thinks of her at all it is as of one who is dead. Life with Margaret is essentially stable, calm and reassuring, and if he never feels for her the passion which he felt for Fanny, he loves her with an affection which is deep and enduring.

Margaret for her part lavishes on him all the love and care which she might have spent on a family of children. Pindlebury is her husband—and also her hobby, a lifetime's occupation. In secret she studies him, makes allowances for him, protects him, perhaps because of an instinctive knowledge that there is one thing she has never meant to him, never could mean. And, because her love makes her intelligent her tactics are never apparent, and Pindlebury is persuaded that *he* is the ruling partner.

So their life goes on and seems as safe and enduring as the country house they live in. Then, one day, the whole structure of it is menaced, and Mr. Pindlebury, who has faced no problems for years, finds himself up against a problem which terrifies him in its enormity.

Fanny has escaped, or more likely is discharged as cured from the sanatorium that has been her prison for so long, and attempts to return to him.

Mr. Pindlebury's first instinct, decided Benvenuto, would be to leave the country, to take Margaret with him away from his resurrected past. So he books passages to America with some half-formed idea that he will settle the affair when he gets to the other side.

Once on board he feels fairly secure—Margaret is still in ignorance of what has happened, and he convinces himself that he can arrange matters so that their life will go on as before.

What was his reaction on finding that Fanny has followed him to the ship, is there beside him waiting to claim her rights?

He makes a secret appointment with her, probably hoping to persuade her to keep silence. He meets her—finds perhaps that for her life has stood still during these thirty years, that she wants, expects, to begin all over again where they had left off. Mr. Pindlebury thinks of his home—thinks of Margaret lying trustfully in her cabin waiting for him. She must never know of this, the shock of it will kill her.

A kind of madness seizes him—the protected becomes the protector—he must save Margaret. And it is so easy. Fanny is standing there alone in the darkness, close to the rail, helpless.

A hand over her mouth—a short struggle, a stifled cry— and it is all over. Mr. Pindlebury creeps away from the rail, back into the life of the ship, back to Margaret. His problem is ended.

Benvenuto rose slowly to his feet. He could find little fault in his own reconstruction, and felt an extreme depression. Poor Margaret Pindlebury, he thought as he began to dress for dinner.

Later, straightening his tie at the mirror before leaving his cabin, he considered himself with some irritation. What had happened to him, why was he finding such difficulty in preserving an impersonal point of view towards the problems before him? His wits were getting blunted with sentiment, he told himself angrily. What were these people to him? Four days ago he had been ignorant of their existence. Now, he caught himself trying to avoid the logical conclusions of his own reasoning. Each one of these strangers had become, for him, a human being whose hopes, fears and sufferings affected him strangely. The dead woman, Samuel Pindlebury, Margaret Pindlebury, Ann—they were no longer people whose probable motives and actions he could analyse coldly and dispassionately. He was being blinded and confused by his own sympathies. It must stop.

Seeking for a reason, he decided to blame the *Atalanta*. It was a spell she had cast on him; the life of the great ship, concentrated and intense, isolated and artificial, had caught him in its toils, robbed him of his sense of proportion, of his ability to exist as a detached observer.

He found himself longing to be ashore again. How could he think clearly in a world where the ground rocked beneath his feet, where the horizon swung like a skipping rope, and wind and water roared in restless fury against the ship's side?

The door of his cabin slammed behind him as he went out, making him jump nervously.

When he reached the bar he found it almost deserted, most of the passengers apparently being confined to their cabins. In a corner he could see Mr. Gowling at his usual table, drinking by himself, while against the bar, perched upon a high stool and twinkling amiably over a glass he held in his hand, was Mr. Pindlebury.

"Come and join me," he called to Benvenuto. "Glad to see you're keeping your sea legs," he went on, as Benvenuto swung on to a stool beside him. "Most people seem as if they can't stand a little breeze. All imagination in my opinion. They think they're going to be sick so they *are* sick. Stuff and nonsense! What'll you have?"

"Gin and bitters, I think—thanks very much. Where's Mrs. Pindlebury? Not feeling the weather, I hope?"

Mr. Pindlebury grunted. "Insists on lying down. Got hold of some new-fangled theory about the balance of liquid behind the ear drums. *I* don't know what she means. I tell her a glass or two in the stomach does more good than any amount in the ears, but she won't listen to reason. You can't argue with a woman. She's not very used to the sea, you know."

"I thought you'd crossed many times," said Benvenuto.

"*I* have. Margaret hasn't. Thought I'd bring her this time for a change of air."

"Will you be staying long?" asked Benvenuto.

"Don't know yet. Depends. Don't waste time talking about us—how are your investigations getting on? Caught your murderer yet?"

Benvenuto shook his head as he put down his empty glass. "It's a difficult job. Have another drink while I tell you about it." He summoned the steward. "Two gin and bitters, please."

He pushed a dish of olives towards Mr. Pindlebury, and taking one himself nibbled it reflectively.

"You'd think on first consideration," he said, "that a murder on board ship would be easy to investigate. You've got your murderer as safe as if he were in prison, without a chance of his escaping until the ship berths. Actually that's a great disadvantage. Nine times out of ten a murderer betrays himself by his attempt to make a get-away. Then again, it's extremely difficult to sum people up when they're divorced from their surroundings. In a ship like this one has very few clues to the normal characters or occupations of the people one meets."

Mr. Pindlebury nodded. "They all look like moneylenders or company promoters to me. Infernal bounders. Go on."

"Well, of course, the worst disadvantage of the lot is that one is cut off from the recourses of Scotland Yard. Most people don't realize the extraordinarily efficient machinery that exists at the Yard for gathering information and sifting evidence. One hears about their failures because the papers seize on them and make a song about them. Personally, if I committed a crime in England, I should be very dubious as to my chances of getting away with it."

"Aren't you making use of the wireless?" inquired Mr. Pindlebury, taking a sip of his drink.

"Of course the wireless is a help—but it all takes time and one's inquiries are bound to be of the hit or miss variety. Another difficulty is that I can't go about taking passengers' finger-prints, or inquiring where they were and what they were doing two nights ago between 10.30 and 11 p.m. I could ask you what *you* were doing because I happen to know you—but what about the next man? He'd be furious and write to the Company about it. Besides—think of the time it would take, testing the statements of about a thousand people."

Benvenuto drank gloomily, then looked across at Mr. Pindlebury. "Have you ever tried," he said, "to make a statement, on oath, about what you were doing at a given time several days previously?"

"Can't say I have," said Mr. Pindlebury, shortly.

"Well I have, and it's extraordinary how difficult it is. Just try to think, for instance, what you were doing two nights ago between half-past ten and eleven."

Mr. Pindlebury removed the stone of an olive from his mouth and reflected, then frowned. "How on earth d'you expect me to remember?" he said testily.

"It's interesting as an experiment," said Benvenuto. "Perhaps I can help. You left us in the dance-room if you remember, and went off to take Mrs. Pindlebury to her cabin—said you'd see me later. The next time I saw you was in the Captain's office, after the murder."

"Oh—it's the night of the murder you're talking about. Of course I know where I was. I was in bed. Got up again when I heard all the shouting."

"There you are," said Benvenuto. "It's quite simple when one begins to link things up. If Mrs. Pindlebury had been here she'd have remembered too."

"No, she wouldn't," snapped Mr. Pindlebury. "She wasn't there. Suddenly took it into her head to take the air, instead of going to sleep like a sensible woman. *I* went to bed. The result was, by the time I'd got my trousers on, the body was found and brought on board. Most annoying. One doesn't see that sort of thing every day."

Benvenuto lit a cigarette and nodded. "It was quite dramatic as a matter-of-fact. Hullo—you're not going to dine yet? Have another drink—"

But Mr. Pindlebury had climbed down from his stool.

"No thank you young man, I never take more than two cocktails—pickles the liver. I must go and see how Margaret's getting on. See you later."

With a rather dry nod Mr. Pindlebury had gone. Benvenuto felt annoyed with himself. Clumsily, he had destroyed Mr. Pindlebury's mood of cheerful expansion. He had no time, however, for self-reproach, for at that moment a hand descended on his arm and he turned to see Mr. Gowling, swaying slightly on his feet and wearing an expression of high good humour.

"Have a drink, ole man," said Mr. Gowling. "You gotta have a drink with me. Never bear malice. *I* don't bear malice. It doesn't do to bear malice."

He seized Benvenuto by the coat lapel and peered into his face with alcoholic gravity. "Always remember that, old man. If ever you feel it coming on say to yourself, 'my old pal Len Gowling told me never to bear—hup—malice.'"

Loosening his grip he spun round, but Benvenuto brought a chair into contact with his straying legs and he sat down suddenly.

"Very good advice, Mr. Gowling," said Benvenuto. "I'll always remember it."

"Tha's right. Let's be frens. You're a good feller—I'm good feller—barman's good feller. Let's all have a drink—"

"I won't have another, thanks. I've got a lot to do this evening. How about a spot of dinner?"

Mr. Gowling rose unexpectedly, to his feet. "You're quite right," he said, "always right. Clever ole man. Lot to do this evening—business—must keep clear head. Remember—'nother time—you drink with me." He slapped his pocket-book and winked. "Plenty of the needful. Fancy you believin' that yarn I told you—" he laughed uproariously and wiped his eyes. "I led you up the garden proper; poor ole man. But remember—no malice!"

He rambled off towards the dining-saloon.

CHAPTER XIX
BED-TIME STORY

THE DINING SALOON was thinly populated, and wore a depressed air. The orchestra, attempting gallantly to distract attention from the rising storm, burst into a Hungarian Rhapsody as Benvenuto entered, but the expressions of the surviving passengers were far from rapturous, and the usual accompaniment of voices and laughter was muted in tone.

Leisurely stewards in attendance upon the few occupied tables performed miracles of balance as they carried trays across the heaving floor, and Benvenuto's own steward greeted him with a pleased smile.

"I was afraid you weren't coming down, sir," he said.

Having ordered clear soup, a grill and some salad, Benvenuto looked about at his fellow diners.

Mr. Gowling was the solitary occupant of his table, and glancing swiftly across the room Benvenuto was relieved to see Lord Stoke, eating his dinner with every appearance of enjoyment.

Where, he wondered, were Ann and Blount? It would be a little unheroic if their high resolve were thwarted by nothing more dignified than *mal de mer*. Still watching Lord Stoke, who was carefully peeling a peach, he noticed an extra steward standing motionless at a few feet from his lordship's chair. The Captain's watch dog was on duty.

His eye next wandered to the Pindleburys' table. Mr. Pindlebury was eating his dinner, but Margaret, Benvenuto noticed with regret, was absent. He hoped she would re-appear during the evening; there was a question he particularly wished to ask her.

By the time he had finished his meal he was the last occupant of the dining saloon—it was already half-past nine. In an hour's time he would be replacing the Captain's bodyguard over Lord Stoke. He went up to the lounge to fortify himself with black coffee.

Looking round for a comfortable seat he saw, sitting on a secluded divan behind a palm tree, Ann Stewart, and with her, his arm lying familiarly along the cushions at her back, his flushed face bent close to her smiling one, Lord Stoke.

Benvenuto started forward impelled by a mixture of feelings—rage, disgust and fear. Then he stopped.

What could he do?

If he approached them he would almost certainly be snubbed by Ann. Worse, they would probably rise and leave him. Here in this room among groups of bridge players, with stewards passing by, with the Captain's watch dog on duty, nothing could happen. Nothing, that was to say, but the fact that Stoke was close to her, breathing into her face, touching her hand with his own.

Feeling slightly sick Benvenuto walked away, found a table and ordered some coffee.

As he sat sipping it and gradually growing calm, he saw Mrs. Pindlebury making her way down the room. She walked slowly, clinging to various pieces of furniture as she came, and looking about her. She was a little pale, but still wore her vague smile. He got up and greeted her.

"Have you seen Pindlebury?" she asked.

"Not since dinner," replied Benvenuto. "Shall I go and fetch him for you?"

"Dear me, no!" said Mrs. Pindlebury, scandalized. "He's probably having a very happy time. Have you forgotten my little confidences?"

"Indeed I haven't. Do please sit down and have a drink with me."

"Well, just for a minute—then I must run along to bed. Isn't it dreadfully rough—it makes me quite giddy. You don't think it will get worse, do you?"

"I expect it will be grand to-morrow. But I'm afraid you won't get your evening walk to-night."

"My evening walk?"

"Yes—don't you generally go round the deck before going to bed?"

Mrs. Pindlebury shook her head vigorously.

"Never! Night air at sea is far too treacherous. What put that into your head?"

"Only that I thought I saw you walking round the deck on the night that poor woman went overboard."

"Dear, no, I went to bed early and was asleep when it happened. I woke up of course when all the shouting began, and bells started ringing—I was dreadfully frightened and called out for Pindlebury, thinking we'd struck an iceberg; but of course he wasn't there—it was quite early. I have always liked keeping early hours, and Pindlebury never has—so unfortunate. I had just got dressed when a nice stewardess came in and told me what had happened. Poor, poor creature. Someone was telling me only to-day that she was mad and jumped overboard in a frenzy."

"No one knows much about her," said Benvenuto. "She was travelling alone."

Mrs. Pindlebury fumbled for her handkerchief. "I can't bear to think of it—such a lonely death and so cold. I only hope I shall die in my bed. I always pray for that—and I pray I shall outlive Pindlebury. I daresay that sounds very queer to you, but he'd be *so* helpless by himself, you know. Dear me, *what* a gloomy conversation! You won't ask me to have a drink again, I'm sure—and this brandy is so delicious, just what I needed. Now I must run along to bed."

She rose from her chair.

"You go and talk to some young people—you're looking quite solemn. There—there's that pretty Lady Stoke. Go and talk to her. Good night, and thank you *so* much."

Benvenuto walked with her to the door, and was hailed by Lady Stoke as he returned.

"Come and cheer me up, for goodness' sake. This place is like a morgue—gives me the creeps, really. Look at those green-faced old men!"

She made a place for him beside her.

"I expect you want cheering up yourself," she went on meaningly.

"Why d'you say that?"

"Well, of course I don't wish to say anything, but I *did* feel sorry for you just now."

She paused again, irritatingly.

He repressed a desire to shake her, then laughed.

"Do tell me what you mean."

"Aren't you the limit—just as if you didn't know all about it. You mustn't think I'm blaming *you*, you know. To tell you the truth, just between you and me, it's a bit of a relief. Keeps him from nosing into my affairs so much. After all, a girl must have a bit of freedom, don't you think? Besides, *you* weren't to know. It's just what I always say, appearances *are* deceptive. I was taken in myself by all that high and mighty touch-me-not air, I don't mind admitting it. You can never tell, with these board-ship pick-ups. But you mustn't worry about *me*, you know."

She took up her mirror and commenced to powder her nose.

"Are you referring," said Benvenuto, controlling his temper with difficulty, "to the fact that Mrs. Stewart is having a drink with your husband?"

Lady Stoke paused, powder-puff in hand, and looked at him. Then she burst out laughing.

"Having a drink! Oh, dear, excuse me. A drink? Aren't you mother's little blue-eyed boy. Why, I've just seen the two of them go into your precious Mrs. Stewart's cabin and lock the door. Drink, indeed! Is that how you usually drink with a girl friend?"

But she got no answer. Benvenuto was rushing from the room, pushing people out of his path. He noticed from the tail of his eye that the divan behind the palm tree was empty.

Fool, he called himself. Fool! Why had he ceased for one moment to watch them?

In the hall both lift gates were closed. A page stepped forward to push the button, but Benvenuto was already halfway up the stairs, stumbling in his haste as the ship lurched sideways.

At the top he paused, clinging to the rail, hesitating. Which one, in this maze of corridors, led to Ann's cabin?

He blundered on, losing himself, then all at once found he was right—there ahead of him was Ann's door. In an instant the handle was in his hand.

But it was locked.

Inside, a gramophone was playing.

CHAPTER XX
DOUBLE CROSSING

"Stop—stop! Let me go! Oh, my God—let me *go*, I tell you!"

The voice was Ann's. Thin, shrill and breaking, it rose above the sound of the gramophone.

Benvenuto, waiting in the darkness of Morton-Blount's empty cabin, started forward.

But before he could reach the door between the two cabins it burst open, and Ann rushed through, banging it behind her, locking and bolting it with frenzied fingers.

Standing in the darkness he could hear her sobbing breath as she stood there, a vague white shape spread-eagled against the door.

He put out his hand and switched on the light. For a moment he thought she would shriek, as her hand flew to her mouth and her eyes stared in terror.

As they faced each other the gramophone ceased in the middle of the tune; they heard footsteps crossing the floor of her cabin, and the outside door being opened and shut.

Suddenly, without quite knowing how, Benvenuto found himself holding Ann in his arms while she clung to him, shuddering and weeping. He didn't say anything, but held her tightly, her hair touching his face.

At last: "Why didn't they come? Why did they leave me alone with him?"

Her body shook violently as her hands gripped his shoulder.

"It was awful—awful! I was alone with him, waiting for them. He took hold of me. I had nothing—you'd taken my gun away."

After a moment she looked up at him, then slipped out of his arms and went and sat on the bed. She was still crying, tears running down her white face. Benvenuto took his handkerchief from his pocket and gave it to her.

"Thank you. I promised Roger and Mr. Gowling I wouldn't do it alone. We were to be three, together. I took him to my cabin, they were to come, directly after. But they didn't come. He—he kissed me. Oh God! I didn't think I could mind about anything ever again. I kept alive, just to do this thing. But when he touched me—it was so hideous—"

The stream of words stopped as she hid her face. When she looked up again her eyes were haunted and desperate.

"And now—the waiting is going to start all over again. It was the only thing I minded, the waiting. Mr. Gowling made us wait, but at last, to-night, we were going to do it. You can't think what it's been like, trying to behave like an ordinary person, and all the time waiting and listening for a signal from the other two. Every time there was a knock on the door I thought it had come—I thought I'd be free—"

As she spoke the door-handle rattled, and Morton-Blount came into the room. He looked nervous and distraught.

"Ann! What have you been doing? I've been waiting all this time—"

"Waiting!" Ann sprang up from the bed shaking with fury.

"It's about all you're good for, Roger, waiting. Why didn't you come, both of you? Why have you let me down? I had him there in my cabin. I saw Mr. Gowling as we came down—he was looking at us—so I knew you'd know when to come. You're cowards and fools, both of you. I shall act alone now. You've failed me, and yourselves too."

"But—Ann!" Morton-Blount looked at her helplessly, almost weeping as the tide of her rage swept over him. "Ann, I *was* ready. I was in the smoking-room, trying to read a paper, and waiting for the signal from Gowling, just as we'd arranged. But he never came! How was I to know what to do? I waited until I couldn't bear it any longer, and then I came down here to see what was happening. Really, Ann, I think you're most unfair."

"I'm sorry, Roger. I—I think I'm tired."

She put her hand to her head and sat down suddenly.

"I still don't understand," she said.

"Perhaps I can explain," said Benvenuto. "I rather think your friend Mr. Gowling is double crossing you."

"Double crossing—" Morton-Blount looked at him in a bewildered fashion, then his face changed as the meaning dawned upon him.

"*Impossible!*" he said violently. "I refuse to hear such an unjust prejudiced suggestion. Leonard Gowling is a man with the highest ideals, and a true love of humanity. Just because he and his kind have been cheated—"

"Shut up," said Benvenuto unkindly. He hurried across the room to Ann, but before he could reach her she slipped sideways off her chair and lay in a heap on the floor.

Quickly he picked her up in his arms.

"Open that door," he said.

Morton-Blount rushed to the door and fumbled clumsily with the bolt. Benvenuto, standing for support against the wall of the swaying cabin, looked down at the face of Ann lying white against his sleeve. In her unconsciousness she looked extraordinarily fragile and helpless, her lovely mouth drooping, her lashes, still wet with tears, curving over the dark shadows beneath her eyes. Slowly and carefully he walked across the swaying floor, through the door held open by Morton-Blount, and into Ann's cabin.

"Ring for the stewardess," he said over his shoulder as he laid her on the bed.

Morton-Blount started nervously and went to the bell, then came and stood looking down at Ann with frightened eyes.

"W-what's the matter with her?" he stammered imploringly at Benvenuto. "She's not—not dying, is she?"

"Of course not—don't be a fool! She's fainted, and no wonder. Go and get some water. Come in—" he added as a knock sounded on the door.

A stout and capable-looking stewardess entered.

"Mrs. Stewart has fainted," said Benvenuto. "Please look after her, and sit with her when she comes round. Ring for the doctor if you think it necessary."

"Dear, dear—poor young lady, how white she is. There's some it takes one way and some another. I've got my hands full to-night, I can tell you. But still I'll send someone in to her if I have to leave. Go along now, both of you."

From Morton-Blount's cabin Benvenuto looked back at the bed. The stewardess was bathing Ann's face and already her eyes were opening.

With a quick movement he went back, shut up the gramophone and pushed it out of sight. Then he followed Morton-Blount into his cabin and shut the door.

"I'm trusting you to stay here and see that Mrs. Stewart does not leave her cabin again to-night, and that she is undisturbed," he said.

"Yes—certainly. Certainly, of course," said Morton-Blount.

Benvenuto left him standing forlornly in the middle of the cabin, clasping and unclasping his hands. He was a pitiful creature in an emergency.

Downstairs in the smoking-room the first person Benvenuto saw as he entered was Mr. Gowling, who was sitting alone at the far end of the room drinking coffee. He was in no mood to talk to Mr. Gowling or anybody else at the moment, and he sat down at an empty table and ordered a drink.

Looking at the clock he saw that it was a quarter to eleven. He had been due to take over the guard on Lord Stoke a quarter of an hour before. However, there was no hurry, he thought, lighting a cigarette. With Ann in bed and Morton-Blount in his cabin, he had time to relax.

Just then a hand descended on his shoulder and he looked up in surprise.

"I want to talk to you, young man," said Lord Stoke.

CHAPTER XXI
THE BLACKMAILER

"SIT DOWN," said Benvenuto, after a pause.

His lordship sat down. He seemed perturbed and looked nervously round. Then, his eye lighting on a steward, he summoned him.

"Bring me a brandy and soda. Oh—er—what about you—what'll you take?"

Benvenuto shook his head, lifting his half-filled glass.

"No, thanks."

Lord Stoke busied himself with a cigar until the steward returned. Then he squirted a very small quantity of soda into his brandy and took a gulp.

"This is a most delicate matter," he began confidentially, leaning across the table until his face was within a foot of Benvenuto's own. "I want you to appreciate that very thoroughly. I take it I have the word of a gentleman—"

Benvenuto raised his eyebrows slightly, and waited. He was feeling very unlike what he took to be Lord Stoke's conception of a gentleman.

"I am sure I can have every confidence in you." His lordship's voice was at once patronizing and oily. "As a matter-of-fact I understand that Sir George Beckworth has already confided in you—without, I may add, asking my permission. However, since making inquiries about you, I feel the affair could not be in better hands."

"Oh—you are talking about the anonymous letter," said Benvenuto, relieved.

"Hush—a little more quietly, please. I have my position to consider."

Benvenuto looked round, but there was no one within earshot.

"Sorry," he said. "What can I do to help you?"

Lord Stoke leant forward and brought his fist down upon the table.

"*I have received another*," he said hoarsely.

Benvenuto nodded. "These people are usually good correspondents. Have you any idea of the author?"

His lordship laughed, an unpleasant sound.

"I have a very good idea," he said, "and I mean to act on it. That is where you can help me. The writer is in this room. Don't turn round for a moment. Now—over there in that corner—the damned scoundrel!"

Benvenuto looked for a moment at the unconscious profile of Mr. Gowling, then back at his lordship's angry face.

"What are you proposing to do?"

"I'll tell you. I have written to the man—his name is Gowling—arranging to meet him in his cabin at eleven o'clock tonight—in a few minutes' time, in fact. He is probably under the impression that I mean to come to terms with him. So I do. But not in the way he expects."

His lordship's face was so unpleasant that Benvenuto felt momentarily sorry for Mr. Gowling. Suddenly, however, it assumed a more benevolent appearance.

"I am not a hard man, Mr. Brown," he said. "I intend to be merciful. Firm, but merciful. I shall confront him with his damned scurrilous letters in the presence of a witness and tell him that if I ever hear from him again I shall turn him over to the police. Since I shall do this in your presence, he will see that I am in earnest."

"Oh—you want me to come with you?"

His lordship's face softened still more. "There are few men, Mr. Brown, in whom I would place sufficient confidence to entrust with so delicate an affair. You can have no idea of the difficulties of a man in my position. With my influence in the Press, my influence, I might add, for Good in the Press of our whole Empire, I am a target—"

But Benvenuto never heard for whom he was a target. A commotion had arisen at the far end of the room, and voices were raised angrily. Benvenuto swung round in his chair to see Morton-Blount, white-faced and apparently in a state of violent agitation, shaking Mr. Gowling by the sleeve.

"I insist on an explanation," he shouted.

"'Ere—'oo are you pulling about?" inquired Mr. Gowling furiously. The discussion, however, got no further, for the drink steward interrupted them.

"Now, now, gentlemen, quietly. No more of that. Outside, *if* you please."

In a moment he had hustled them both out on to the deck, Morton-Blount still clinging to Mr. Gowling's sleeve.

Lord Stoke walked to the door and looked after them, then returned to his table.

"You see the kind of man he is," he remarked. "Makes enemies wherever he goes." He shook his head sadly.

"The blackmailer is a pestiferous crawling coward, able to throw mud at the fair name of any upright man who is in a high position. And mud sticks, Mr. Brown, it sticks. One must be firm. If I were not such a foolish tender-hearted old fellow I should turn him over to the law. But who knows—perhaps there is a little seed of goodness even in that black heart. I like to think so. I like to think I am giving a fellow creature another chance. Your presence at this interview will show him that I don't fear his lying threats, and will prevent his attempting any violence."

"All right," said Benvenuto, "I'll come with you."

"I see it is eleven o'clock," said Lord Stoke, "let me just show you the letter before we face him with it."

He felt in his pocket, and his face clouded with a dark scowl of anger.

"Damn that blockhead of a valet of mine—he's forgotten my pocket-book again. If you'll wait here a moment, Mr. Brown, I'll go and get it."

His lordship hurried from the room, with remarkable agility considering the increasing violence of the ship's motion. Benvenuto watched him bobbing across the floor, then turned to finish his drink. As he set it down he saw Lady Stoke appear in a doorway opposite to the one by which her husband had left. She looked round the room, and seeing Benvenuto crossed over to him.

"Have you seen Stokey?"

"He's just gone."

"Well, thank goodness. Here, wait a minute—I'll be back."

She hurried to the door and signalled to someone in the passage, then waited, steadying herself against the wall.

Rutland King's entrance was spectacular. He appeared in the archway, one hand smoothing waved locks from his pale brow, the other thrust Napoleonically into the opening of his dinner jacket, and paused, as though allowing invisible cameras time to click. Unfortunately the ship chose this moment for a particularly violent roll, and the screen lover, putting out his hand a second late, reeled forward into the arms of Benvenuto who had followed Lady Stoke to the door. He collapsed into a chair and looked as if he were about to cry.

"I wish this bally boat would keep *still*. Sylvia, *why* wouldn't you let me stay in my cabin? This is insufferable."

"Oh, darling, I am sorry. Let's all have a little drinky and forget about it."

"I'm afraid I can't," said Benvenuto. "I'm waiting for your husband—he's just coming back to fetch me."

The effect upon Rutland King was galvanic; he was out of his chair and through the doorway in an instant. Lady Stoke turned angrily to Benvenuto.

"Why ever couldn't you say so before? I'd never have brought Rutland in here. Now look what you've done! He's so sensitive, this will upset him for days—"

"I'm very sorry—" he began, but she had gone, hurrying after her star.

Whatever else life in the *Atalanta* might be, decided Benvenuto, it wasn't dull. It was a little difficult to decide whether the main *motif* were tragedy or farce—but it was certainly a production in which the entries and exits were perfectly timed, he thought, turning back to his table and seeing Lord Stoke coming towards him. The boat had one clear advantage over the legitimate stage, since its motion gave to the movements of all the characters a definitely slap-stick effect. His lordship, for example, was advancing with a purposeful and bad-tempered expression on his face, which was more than counteracted by his wild and uncertain progress across the heaving floor.

"Confound the storm," he said breathlessly, clinging to a table for support. "Damnably unsteady boat. Here's the letter. Care to look at it before we go?"

"No," said Benvenuto. "I don't want to read it. We'd better get along—we're late."

Lord Stoke swallowed the remainder of his brandy and soda.

"I'm ready," he said.

CHAPTER XXII
RENDEZVOUS

LORD STOKE rapped again, impatiently, upon Mr. Gowling's door. Then he turned the handle and precipitated himself into the lighted cabin.

"The scoundrel's not here," he said.

Benvenuto followed him in and shut the door.

"I expect he's still arguing with Morton-Blount. They looked as if they had a number of things to say to each other. Shall we wait?"

Lord Stoke hesitated, fuming. Then he dragged up a chair and sat down, his fingers drumming on the table. Benvenuto sat opposite to him and drew out his cigarette case, then paused, sniffing the air. The cabin, with its porthole battened against the storm, was stuffy and smelt of stale cigar smoke, and of something else, something which emanated, he decided, from a bottle of disinfectant which lay smashed in the wash-basin.

It was curious, he thought, taking out and lighting a cigarette, how the personality of its occupier affected each cabin. The furnishings upon this deck were more or less uniform in character, or, to be more exact, in lack of character, for steel, glass, wood, and textiles, all were shaped and patterned as though their designers laboured under a frightful fear of being thought old-fashioned. The results, he decided, were depressing, and wore an air of timidity together with one of determination to do the right thing.

Ann's cabin he remembered only as something scented warm and friendly, vaguely silken and feminine. Morton-Blount's wore a slightly academic air and smelt of pipe smoke and the pages of new books. Here, in Mr. Gowling's cabin, there was an oddly bleak and futile atmosphere, which allowed the neo-art shapes of the furniture to insist, irritatingly. Upon the wall facing Benvenuto hung a mirror innocent of frame, its corners zoned in senseless echo of modern American building laws; the table at which he sat, an over-solid mass of unpolished walnut with blunted corners, was too low for comfort; the two arm-chairs were fashioned of tortured steel tubes and rough canvas, and one of them swayed dangerously under the irritable fidgeting of Lord Stoke. Lying across the bed was Mr. Gowling's monstrously patterned dressing-gown keeping company with some shabby pink and white flannel pyjamas; it screamed protestingly at the restrained printed linen bed-hangings, but, at least, thought Benvenuto, it looked human in its cheap provincialism.

He turned to look at Lord Stoke, who had risen to his feet and was pressing his thumb firmly on to the bell, while with his other hand he gripped a piece of furniture to steady himself upon the heaving floor.

"Have you seen Mr. Gowling?" demanded Lord Stoke when the steward answered his summons.

"No, my lord—not since he dressed for dinner."

"Well, go and look for him. Or send a messenger to look for him and fetch me a couple of brandies and sodas. And be quick about it."

"Very good, my lord."

"Twenty minutes late," shouted his lordship across the table to Benvenuto, his voice rising angrily above the noise of the storm. By now the little cabin heaved and pitched in alarming fashion, the walls creaking, the water dashing against the porthole, and every loose object in Mr. Gowling's possession rattling and sliding. At one moment the *Atalanta* held herself tense and still, at the next a vast wave sent her reeling off her balance and her screw, emerging from the water, shook her whole structure in a deep fearful shudder.

Benvenuto lit another cigarette. He felt depressed, and his nerves were frayed by the perpetual movement and noise. He watched a piece of soap sliding back and forth across the wash-basin; listened to an insistent thud from the wardrobe where a suit-case or a pair of shoes kept knocking against the door, and lacked energy to go and silence it. It made a kind of accompaniment to a monologue which Lord Stoke, loudly, was delivering.

"All my life I have been punctilious—" thump thump bang—"in the matter of appointments. One of the secrets of success is a respect for Time." Thump—thump—"It is a copy-book maxim that Time is Money—and how true it is. You will find that it is the small man"—thump bang bang—"the man without vision, who neglects—"

Benvenuto's attention wandered. The sense of gloom and foreboding which had oppressed him before dinner had returned with redoubled intensity, and his thoughts turned to the Pindleburys and finally to Ann. At this moment she was probably, he thought, lying in her cabin only a few yards away, listening to the storm, a stewardess watching by her bed. At this moment she was in no possible danger, he assured himself. No harm could possibly come to her so long as the gross and unatttractive person of Lord Stoke was under his, Benvenuto's, eye. There seemed no reason for his growing uneasiness; he searched his mind, sought an excuse for himself. He disliked this intangible sense of horror or fear, knowing from experience that it usually constituted a danger signal.

Both he and Lord Stoke started nervously as a sharp rap sounded on the door. But it was the steward, carrying a tray. Lord Stoke signed a chit and took up his glass.

"Have you sent someone to look for Mr. Gowling?"

"Yes, my lord. I have sent a page round the public rooms."

"Well, go yourself as well. Here, take this—" he flung a coin down on to the tray and turned to Benvenuto, raising his glass.

"Your very good health, Mr. Brown. I am sorry to keep you waiting like this. I suppose the rascal is having difficulty with that other fellow who spoke to him in the bar. Another victim, do you think?"

Benvenuto smiled. "I can hardly imagine anyone blackmailing Morton-Blount—unless he has been discovered to be a secret member of the Primrose League."

Lord Stoke grunted. "In my opinion this man Gowling is a lunatic. Read this. I need hardly say that I haven't the slightest idea what he is driving at."

He took the letter from his pocket and passed it across the table to Benvenuto. It was roughly printed in the coarse characters of the first letter, and read:

"This is your last chance. Unless you agree to see me and hand me £10,000 your penalty will be exposure and Death before the voyage ends. Be warned this time. I shall not give you another chance."

"What exactly," asked Benvenuto, folding the letter and handing it back, "led you to suppose that the writer of the first letter was Mr. Gowling?"

"I recognized him. He had been hanging about my London office and pestering me as I entered my car. Obviously a lunatic. He appears to think he has sent some priceless invention to me that is to revolutionize industry—a common enough form of mania. Believe me, Mr. Brown, with the large and varied interests that I control I should have to employ a special staff of clerks to deal with the mass of begging letters that are sent to me."

Bump—bump—bang! From the wardrobe the irritating noise went on. Benvenuto could stand it no longer, and got up impatiently to put a stop to it.

But the *Atalanta* chose this moment for a monstrous frolic with the water. She heaved herself upwards, and seemed to shake with infernal glee as her screw left the water and she hung for an instant above the boiling waves. But her triumph was short-lived. Down, down she went, deep into a dark and slippery cavern, falling further and further sideways as a mountain of water thrust itself against her walls. Benvenuto staggered backwards, his stomach seeming to dissolve in space. He was angry now, furious at this senseless movement which defied his efforts to cross the floor, and hurled him back against the cabin wall. He eyed the wardrobe in front of him pugnaciously, ready to plunge forward when the floor straightened.

But he had no need to cross the floor.

As the *Atalanta* slid still further into her watery pit the wardrobe door gave with a click and burst open; with a sickening sliding rush something rolled out of the doorway, on to the carpet, towards Benvenuto's feet. Something that was a limp black-clothed body.

Mr. Gowling had kept his appointment.

CHAPTER XXIII
MURDER

"HULLO—*hullo*—"

Lord Stoke, his face robbed of its usual rosy hue and wearing an expression of shock and horror, rattled the telephone impatiently. He was standing beside the table in Mr. Gowling's cabin, his back turned to where Benvenuto and the steward were kneeling on the floor.

"Is that you, operator? Put me through to the medical officer immediately. Yes. It's urgent."

He paused, the telephone to his ear, and half turned to look at the men at work behind him.

"Hullo—is that you, Doctor? This is Lord Stoke. I am speaking from Cabin 27 D. deck. There's a man been found shot in this cabin—one of the passengers—name of Gowling. Can you come along? What? Oh, yes, I'm afraid so. Yes. Through the head. Cabin 27 D. deck. Right."

He replaced the receiver and stood aside as Benvenuto and the steward moved slowly across to the bed. Then he sat down suddenly and mopped his brow.

"God, why doesn't this ship keep *still* for a minute," he said.

Benvenuto grunted. "You'd better ring through to Markham, the ship's detective. Tell him to inform the Captain, and to come along at once."

Lord Stoke lifted the receiver again. He looked glad to have something to do.

Benvenuto straightened himself from the bed over which he had been bending. The monstrously patterned dressing-gown now hid from view that which had once been Mr. Gowling.

"You'd better clear out—and get yourself a drink," he said in a low voice to the steward. Lord Stoke was speaking into the telephone.

"Gawd!" whispered the steward, "I shan't be sorry when we gets into dock. That's two of 'em gone—and they can't say this one went and fell overboard by accident, neither. Poor little bleeder! Wot's the *matter* with this voyage, sir? Makes you wonder who's going next?"

"Nonsense," said Benvenuto. "Here, take this—and go and have a drink. And keep your mouth shut, see? I don't want this to get about yet."

The man pocketed his half-crown and went out, mopping his brow. Lord Stoke put down the receiver and looked at Benvenuto.

"The inspector is coming along. What did that fellow say? Makes you wonder who's going next—Brown!" He gripped Benvenuto's arm with a shaking hand. His face was not pleasant to see. "Do you realize what this means? That—that—on the bed—he warned me there was a plot to murder me. This is what he's got for it. They'll—they'll get me next—d'you hear? D'you hear?"

"For God's sake be quiet," Benvenuto wrenched at the hand on his arm and flung it on to the table as if it were some inanimate object. "Pull yourself together, can't you? Here's the doctor."

The doctor nodded briefly to the two men, put his bag of instruments down on the table and crossed to the bed. Presently he looked up.

"Nothing to be done to *him*. Where d'you find him? He only seems to have been dead about half an hour."

"In the wardrobe," said Benvenuto briefly.

"*What?* Then—it can't have been suicide. A man wouldn't—"

"No," said Benvenuto, "a man wouldn't put himself away in his wardrobe and then shoot himself."

"Of course it wasn't suicide," shouted Lord Stoke. "It was murder—there's a murderer on board, and it's me he's after!"

"What's all this?" said a voice from the doorway. Inspector Markham walked into the cabin, switched on an extra light, and surveyed the scene before him. He looked extraordinarily solid and reassuring, as if he'd just walked in off his beat.

"A job for you this time, I'm afraid, Markham," said Benvenuto.

The inspector joined the doctor by the bed.

"Only just got it, hasn't he, Doctor? Thought so. Who found him?"

"I did. Lord Stoke and I. We were in here, waiting for him." Benvenuto described briefly what had happened. When he had finished the inspector walked quickly to the wardrobe and groped inside.

"There's no gun," said Benvenuto. "I looked."

"Who occupies that cabin, d'you know?" The inspector pointed to the communicating door.

"A friend of Gowling's called Morton-Blount."

"A friend of Gowling's—" echoed Markham. He went towards the door. "Will you all wait here?" he said.

"Let me come with you," said Benvenuto, "I know him."

The inspector's grunt might have meant assent; Benvenuto took it to mean such and joined him at the door. It was bolted, but bolted upon their own side. The inspector took a flash-lamp from his pocket and examined the handle and the bolt.

"Wiped clean," he said. Then he slid back the bolt and walked in, Benvenuto beside him.

Morton-Blount was sitting in an arm-chair, dressed in a long black dressing-gown, his head bowed in his hands. As he got up and faced them he looked, thought Benvenuto inconsequently, absurdly like Sherlock Holmes. He blinked at them.

"Ah—it is you, Brown. I don't think I know—"

"I am Inspector Markham," said the inspector briskly. "There's a few questions I'd like to ask you."

Morton-Blount passed his hand over his brow and blinked again.

"Certainly," he said faintly. "Won't you sit down? Do you mind if I do—I feel rather unwell." He collapsed suddenly into his chair as the ship rolled. He looked extremely pale.

"How long have you been in here?" asked the inspector.

"Really—I don't know. Perhaps half an hour, perhaps an hour."

"Did you hear anything unusual?"

"No, I don't think so. How could I hear anything in this storm? Why, is anything wrong?"

The inspector glared at him. It was impossible to contradict him about the storm; it beat against the porthole in savage fury, made the ship's timbers strain and creak. It was necessary to raise one's voice in an ordinary conversation.

"Come with me," said the inspector suddenly.

A rather mulish look crossed Morton-Blount's white face.

"I wish you would defer this conversation to another time," he said. "I should like to be undisturbed. I do not wish to move."

"You'd better come, Blount," said Benvenuto.

Morton-Blount got to his feet and looked nervously at the door into Gowling's cabin. The inspector had opened it and stood waiting for him. Very unwillingly Morton-Blount walked forward.

Benvenuto was behind him as he went into the cabin. He watched his tall gaunt figure go into the centre of the room, watched him turn to look at the bed. There was a curious kind of choking gasp, and Morton-Blount came rushing towards him, cannoned into him, beat wildly against him with his hands as he struggled by, then disappeared through the doorway, banging the door behind him.

"Here—" began the inspector.

"I should let him go," said Benvenuto. "He won't move, I promise you."

There was obviously some truth in this statement, and Markham nodded, rather bad-temperedly.

"Well, I must go and report to the Captain. He won't leave the bridge to-night. If you gentlemen would go up to the Captain's office I'll take your statements there, in a few minutes. Thank you, Doctor, there is no need for you to come, I'll see you later. Will you tell them to take this," he jerked his thumb over his shoulder, "to the mortuary. I shan't keep you more than a few minutes, m'lord. Mr. Brown will show you the way."

The inspector went briskly out of the cabin. Lord Stoke rose eagerly from his chair and put his hand on Benvenuto's arm.

"For God's sake let's go and get a drink before we have any more of this."

"No, thanks," said Benvenuto absently. He went out into the corridor, leaving the doctor giving instructions to the steward.

"Brown!" A trembling hand was laid on his arm again. "Wait a minute. There's no hurry. Come with me to the bar— I—I'm shaken. I must have a drink. I don't like this, I tell you—I don't like it!"

All the oiliness had gone from Lord Stoke's voice; he spoke in a thin and tremulous whine. He was rather a horrible sight, thought Benvenuto, looking at him. Shed of his bullying arrogance he was a pricked bladder of a man, a weak cringing coward. Pomposity had suited him better.

"All right," said Benvenuto. "I'll come."

When they got there it was deserted, except for two stewards, who were having a drink behind the bar. One of them came swiftly forward and served Lord Stoke with a double brandy. He drank it down in one gulp and felt for his cigar case.

"That's better," he said. "That was the most ghastly experience I've ever had in my life. To think that all the time we were there, waiting for him—" he shuddered.

"I didn't enjoy it, either," said Benvenuto.

"It's a different matter for you," said Lord Stoke. "Don't you see what this means? Don't you understand the danger—"

Benvenuto raised a warning hand. Lord Stoke looked at him, then pushed his glass across the bar for another drink.

"Excuse me, sir," said the steward, pouring brandy into a fresh glass, "is it true there's been another murder?"

"A man has been found shot," said Benvenuto. "What d'you mean, another murder?"

"Well, it was queer about that other party, wasn't it, sir, if you don't mind my saying so? They've been saying, down below, that that was no suicide, nor accident neither. Someone pushed 'er in. She was an eccentric old party, I know, sir, but her stewardess says she'd never have gone and done a thing like that. Quite made friends with her, it seems. And it *can't* 'ave been an accident, sir. The sea was flat, not like it is to-night—and people don't go falling off the *Atalanta* by accident. It's queer to say the least, isn't it, sir, if you'll pardon me?"

The man looked nervously across at Benvenuto, afraid he had been talking too much.

"I shouldn't take too much notice of what they say," said Benvenuto, taking a light for his cigarette. "Nobody knows the rights of this new business yet. The man may have shot himself."

Lord Stoke had drunk his second brandy and his face was flushed.

"Why try to hush it up?" he demanded loudly. "There's a murderer on board and you know it."

"I think," said Benvenuto, "that if you're ready we'd better go. Good night, steward."

"Good night, sir."

"Have you ever been in a ship where there's a panic?" inquired Benvenuto, as they walked along the deserted corridor. "*I* have, once in the Pacific. It wasn't pleasant."

"I don't care a damn if it's pleasant or not," said Lord Stoke. "I'm in danger of my life, and the more people that know it, the better. I must be protected. You don't seem to realize—"

Benvenuto sighed as his lordship went on. He sighed again later in the Captain's office as Lord Stoke recounted to Markham the story of Gowling's threats, and impressed upon him what he took to be the significance of Gowling's death. Markham, Benvenuto could see, was half-impressed. Well—Lord Stoke might be right.

Presently Benvenuto got up. "I don't think there's any more I can tell you, Markham. If you want me again I'll be in my cabin."

"Thank you, Mr. Brown, but I think I can get along all right. I'll soon have my hands on whoever did it, don't you worry, sir. Good night."

It was, reflected Benvenuto, Markham's hour of triumph. The professional replacing the amateur. Well, he hadn't done much himself towards solving the problem of Miss Smith, he thought, going down to his cabin. He wondered when the answer would come to his wireless to Scotland Yard.

CHAPTER XXIV
OLD LADIES

BENVENUTO BROWN sat down at the table in his cabin and spread some sheets of note-paper in front of him. He wrote:

Reasons why there is a probability of some connection between the murders of Miss Smith and Mr. Gowling.

(1)The lives of Miss Smith and Mr. Gowling were in some way linked before they came aboard the *Atalanta*. I state this

(*a*)because she evinced an interest in him.

(*b*)because he fainted upon seeing her body, and

(*c*)because he protested too much his lack of knowledge of her.

(NOTE: Answer to my wireless to Scotland Yard may cast some light on this.)

(2)It is, to say the least, unlikely that one transatlantic line should carry at a time more than one active and able-bodied murderer, and be the scene of two totally dissociated crimes.

(NOTE: Possibly a conventional point of view but the result of, I think, a sound instinct.)

He frowned heavily at what he had written, took a fresh sheet of note-paper, and began again.

Why should Anyone Wish to Murder Mr. Gowling?

Ruling out the obvious irritants such as his personality, clothes, manners, etc. with which he existed unmolested for a good many years, I have:

(1)Lord Stoke's theory that Mr. Gowling was eliminated by the party or parties who are plotting against his, Lord Stoke's, life, on account of his treachery, or—

(2)The possibility that Mr. Gowling's end was in consequence of over-indulgence in the exercise of his new profession, i.e., blackmail. Is it not possible that, having started to blackmail Lord Stoke he got a taste for it, and that either—

(a)he recognized somebody on board whom he knew had some previous connection with Miss Smith; concluded that this person was responsible for her death; attempted to blackmail him or her, and was murdered by him or her, or—

(b)he accidentally came upon a clue as to the identity of Miss Smith's murderer, and attempted blackmail with the same result.

(3)The possibility of the existence of some person unknown, to whom Mr. Gowling's continued existence was a nuisance, or a danger. I must not lose sight of this idea simply because I do not fancy a brand new and dissociated plot.

There may be no link between Miss Smith's death and Mr. Gowling's death.

Benvenuto's expression became more and more dissatisfied. He took a third sheet of paper and recommenced.

What is to be deduced from the fact that Mr. Gowling was killed, in mid-ocean by a shot from a revolver?

(1)The probability that he was shot by someone who came aboard prepared to commit murder.

(2)That he was shot by someone who came aboard in a desperate state of mind contemplating suicide, or—

(3)By someone who carries a revolver because he feared attack—or—

(4)That he was merely shot by someone who habitually travelled with a gun.

(5)That he was shot by someone who stole or borrowed a gun for the purpose.

(NOTE: Reasons 1 and 2 seem the most likely.)

List of persons who came aboard prepared to commit murder:

(1)Ann Stewart.

(2)Roger Morton-Blount.

(3)Mr. Gowling himself.

(4)Any one of the rest of the passengers, unknown to me.

Persons who came aboard in a desperate frame of mind, contemplating suicide—

Benvenuto paused for several minutes. Then he wrote underneath:

Samuel Pindlebury?

He put all three sheets of paper in front of him and stared at them. But he was not reading them.

Why had Mr. Pindlebury lied to him about his movements on the night of Miss Smith's death? He had said that he was in bed at the time of the alarm and had got up and dressed too late to see the rescue.

Mrs. Pindlebury, on the other hand, had said that she was alone in her cabin at the time of the alarm, that she had called for Pindlebury only to find he was not there. One of them was lying. And there was no reason for her to lie. No, there was no reason—

Benvenuto, quite suddenly, put his hands over his face. It was not a pleasant picture that had flashed across his brain.

"No," he said loudly, into the empty cabin.

Her hands were white and dimpled, amongst the tangle of pink wool. Her hair net had blown sideways in the wind, so that she looked absurdly rakish. She smelled warmly and comfortably of lavender-water and furs. She was the epitome of all the nice old ladies he had ever known, old ladies who put on gardening gloves and went off to pluck dead blossoms from the rose bushes, old ladies who brewed the tea themselves over a shining paraphernalia of tea caddies and spirit lamps, old ladies who loved dogs and cats and children, old ladies who held out their spiritual umbrellas to anyone needing shelter.

Benvenuto shifted restlessly in his chair. He felt as if he had filthily insulted one of his old aunts. Violently he attempted to eradicate from his mind a picture of Mrs. Pindlebury, sending Miss Smith down into the dark water.

All her life she has protected Pindlebury, said a voice in his brain.

But old ladies don't go about doing things like that, he told himself.

And suppose that trouble or disgrace threaten someone they love, someone whose self-appointed protectors they are, what do old ladies do then? Do they fight to the last ditch to keep their spiritual umbrellas unfurled, do they even commit murder to do it? Once he had known an old gentleman who murdered for the sake of his son he thought, remembering Major Kent and Adrian. He could understand that.

How much strength and ruthlessness lay behind the world that the old ladies had built up, the world of flowers and tea-cups and firelit drawing-rooms?

His eyes, staring gloomily at the table top, came to rest on the heading of his first sheet of notes. "Reasons why there is a probability of some connection between the murders of Miss Smith and Mr. Gowling."

Well, he thought with impatient relief, no old lady killed Mr. Gowling. She wouldn't have had the strength to lift his body and put it in a wardrobe. He was glad to think of some perfectly logical and obvious reason to pit against an idea that was as fantastic as it was distasteful.

He was back to his original question. Why had Mr. Pindlebury lied? He would have to see him, he decided, make him talk.

He looked again at his notes. "Persons who came aboard prepared to commit murder. *Ann Stewart.* Yes, he thought. She had the strength, and the determination to use it. He got up and looked in a suit-case where he had put Ann's gun. It was still there. That, he thought, would be no obstacle to her. Morton-Blount probably had a gun, Gowling also. He thought of Ann's tense white face, her repressed hysteria, her extraordinary air of being ruled by one indomitable purpose. Would she have allowed Gowling to stand in the way of her revenge? Would she have killed him if she suspected him of the intention to betray her?

He got up and looked at his watch. It was after midnight. It doesn't matter what time it is, he thought. To-morrow is the last full day at sea. He would go and see her.

He locked his notes into a suit-case and made his way along to D. deck. The storm was subsiding. The ship seemed deserted.

He tapped on Ann's door, then tapped again, louder. But there was no answer. Cautiously he pushed it open. The cabin was lighted, but the stewardess he had left on guard had gone, and Ann had gone. He paused a moment, then entered, shut the door, and rang the bell for the stewardess.

When she came and saw him standing there in Ann's cabin, she gave a scream.

"It's all right," said Benvenuto, smiling. "Don't you remember me? I asked you to stay with Mrs. Stewart this evening and look after her."

"Excuse me, sir." She was an elderly woman, and her rather plain and sensible face had gone a curious grey. She sat down suddenly on a chair. "It's awful, sir, being up on this corridor, where it happened. Every time I get a ring I go with my heart in my mouth, for fear there's somebody else gone. There's Death lurking in this ship, sir, God help us all. You gave me such a fright, standing there when I expected to find Mrs. Stewart."

"You mustn't get jumpy," said Benvenuto. "The women passengers will depend on people like you, you know. Just tell me this—what time did you leave Mrs. Stewart? She ought not to have got up again to-night."

"I couldn't do anything with her, sir, she would get up though she looked dreadfully white and queer. Sent me off about a quarter to eleven, and said she was going to a friend's cabin. I put a warm coat on her, and I thought maybe it would be better for her to go and talk to someone, she looked that queer and haunted like. Almost as if she knew what was going to happen, sir. Poor lady—there's some people that have got second sight, and know when there's evil about, sir. There's evil about now, God save us!"

"She didn't say whose cabin she was going to?"

"No, sir."

"Thank you, stewardess. There's nothing else. Don't go worrying yourself—I expect you've got your hands full this weather, haven't you? You keep a cool head on you, and you'll prevent the passengers getting panicky."

"Yes, sir. Thank you kindly, sir."

When she had gone Benvenuto tapped on the communicating door to Morton-Blount's cabin. A curious kind of groan answered him. He slipped back the bolt and entered.

"Hullo, Blount—feeling better?"

"Go away," said Morton-Blount.

"I will. Just tell me this. When did you last see Ann?"

"Go away," said Morton-Blount.

Benvenuto went across and shook him by the shoulder.

"It will be a lot easier for you, and quicker, if you tell me when you last saw Ann."

"I haven't seen her. I haven't seen her since you saw her yourself. Now will you *go away*?"

"Thanks. You'll feel better in the morning."

"*Go—*" began Morton-Blount, but Benvenuto had shut the door.

He went quickly along the corridor and down the stairs. He had decided to go to the Pindleburys' cabin.

"Come in," called Mrs. Pindlebury. He went in, an apology on his lips. But Mrs. Pindlebury had not gone to bed. She was sitting on a sofa, and next to her, very tired and white, was Ann.

CHAPTER XXV
PLATINUM BLONDE

"Dear Mr. Brown!" Mrs. Pindlebury was all nods and smiles. "Now come and sit down and tell us all about it. We have really felt quite nervous, sitting here. Our stewardess came in just now and was quite hysterical, poor creature, *insisted* that people were being murdered in their beds. Ann wanted to go and find out, but I simply refused to be left. It *is* all nonsense, isn't it?"

"I'm afraid not," said Benvenuto, sitting down beside her. "I thought you would have heard, Ann. I'm sorry to tell you— Mr. Gowling is dead."

"Mr. Gowling—*dead?*" Her voice was the merest whisper.

"Yes. He was found shot, in his cabin. Found by me, as a matter-of-fact. There is no doubt it was murder."

He thought she was going to faint again. Instead she sat up very straight, a curious light in her eyes, her hands twisting together.

"Poor creature—oh, poor little creature!" murmured Mrs. Pindlebury in shocked tones. "You mean that dreadfully unpleasant little man with drooping moustaches? I thought so. Oh dear, I thought him so repellent, and that always makes it much worse, don't you think? One always feels—if he had lived he *might* have improved. Dear, dear me. Life is very terrible. Now they are saying that poor woman who went overboard was murdered, too. The stewardess says so. I *hope* that isn't true, though really perhaps it is better than believing she threw herself in."

"It's quite true," said Benvenuto.

Mrs. Pindlebury was mopping her eyes with a linen handkerchief.

"Really, one would think we were in America already," she said. She turned round briskly and faced him.

"Now, what wicked person is going about killing all these people? We must find out. Why, I remember now, Pindlebury told me you were a detective! *Isn't* that lucky? You must let me help you. I have the most wonderful instincts about people, haven't I, Ann? Now let me see—" She paused, her eyes very bright. Then: "Of course!" she said. "*I* know. *Lord Stoke.*"

"Why Lord Stoke?" inquired Benvenuto, startled.

"Don't you see—it's *just* the sort of man he is! I knew a man once before who had rolls of flesh on the back of his neck like that, and he was dreadfully unkind to his hunters. I reported him to a Society but they took *no* action. Now, you watch him carefully. I shouldn't be surprised if he committed both the murders."

"There isn't," said Benvenuto, "a scrap of evidence to connect him with Miss Smith."

Suddenly Ann spoke. "There's plenty of evidence to connect him with Mr. Gowling," she said in a strained voice.

Benvenuto shook his head. "It's an admirable idea," he said, "but unfortunately Lord Stoke was with me. And—while he was with me, Mr. Gowling went off with Morton-Blount who was apparently in a tearing passion with him. That is the last time Gowling was seen alive."

Ann jumped to her feet.

"What are you suggesting? Leave poor Roger out of it. You ought to be able to see—"

She stopped, her hand to her mouth, and stared at him.

"I ought to be able to see that Roger Morton-Blount is quite incapable of committing murder," said Benvenuto quietly. "I agree with you—by himself he is quite incapable of it. If he were under the influence of an entirely ruthless character, stronger than his own, I'm not so sure. It would be rather unfair of anyone to try to make him, wouldn't it?"

Over Mrs. Pindlebury's head his eyes met hers, steadily. It was a curious silent duel, cold and bitter. He felt as though he were whipping her, deliberately flaying her skin. His pulses began to beat heavily and violently because her stricken white face was so beautiful. Then she lowered her eyes and turned away. For a moment, in the midst of his problems, he felt cheerful.

For the first time he felt that he had done something towards shaking Ann's purpose.

His thoughts were interrupted by Mrs. Pindlebury. "Of course it wasn't poor Mr. Blount," she was saying. "He wouldn't *dream* of doing such a thing. But if it isn't him, and it isn't Lord Stoke, who *is* the murderer?"

They all three turned at the sound of the door opening. There, in the threshold, stood Mr. Pindlebury. For the second time that night Benvenuto thought of a play in which the entrances and exits were timed with a feeling for stage craft.

"God bless my soul, are you having a party, Margaret? I thought you'd be asleep hours ago. Are you feeling better now that the storm's dropped?"

"Very well indeed, Pindlebury. We were just discussing the murders."

"Murders? So you know all about it, do you? Damnable affair—the whole ship's in a panic. Can't get a steward to answer a bell, all gossiping in corners. People losing their heads. What are the rights of the case, Brown?"

He sat down and looked at Benvenuto, screwing in his eye-glass. It winked in the light, giving him a slightly wicked air. A malevolent mummy, thought Benvenuto.

"There's not much to tell. This man Leonard Gowling was found shot in his cabin, in circumstances that point conclusively to murder. Lord Stoke and I discovered the body. That's all I know. Whether or not this has anything to do with the murder of Miss Smith, I don't know—yet."

"Extraordinary," commented Mr. Pindlebury. "Perfectly extraordinary. Well, it will keep you busy, Brown—your speciality—h'm?"

Benvenuto shook his head. "It's not my affair, this time. Markham is in charge. I expect he'll have all the passengers on the mat to-morrow."

"Damned annoying and unpleasant thing," said Mr. Pindlebury. "I wish to Heaven we'd taken the *Olympic*. However—"

"By a curious coincidence," said Benvenuto, "everyone who is known to have been on speaking terms with Mr. Gowling is, with the exception of Lord Stoke and Morton-Blount, now in this cabin. I was thinking it would save you all a great deal of trouble and unpleasantness if you tell me now what you were each doing between eleven and eleven fifteen to-night, and I'll see Markham first thing in the morning and explain to him."

"What a good idea," said Mrs. Pindlebury brightly. "And quite exciting, like that horrible murder game we used to play. I shall never have the heart to play it again. I'll get you a pencil and paper."

But Mr. Pindlebury was going slowly purple.

"Stuff and nonsense," he said. "I refuse to be questioned by Markham or anybody else. Just because some fellah who never said a civil word to me in his life goes and gets murdered—"

"Now, now, Pindlebury," said his wife. "Here's a pencil and paper, Mr. Brown. Begin with Ann."

"Where were you at the time?" he asked Ann.

"She was with me," said Mrs. Pindlebury swiftly. "She's been with me all the evening, at least ever since you gave me that nice glass of brandy."

Ann smiled faintly. "It's no good, Margaret. Mr. Brown saw me after that. No. I've got no alibi." She looked mockingly at Benvenuto. "During the critical time I was standing all alone on the lee side of the ship watching the storm. Nobody saw me so far as I know. It was a mad thing to do, and I got soaked. You may feel my coat."

She came and stood close to him, her coat on her arm, still looking at him with her curious veiled eyes.

Her coat was wet.

"I haven't got a what-d'you-may-call-um, either," said Mrs. Pindlebury with spirit. "I was in here by myself, lying down. And it can't have been both of us, Mr. Brown."

"That," said Benvenuto smiling, "is an argument that ought to carry weight with Markham. You'd rather talk to Markham, sir?"

Mr. Pindlebury appeared to be at boiling point.

"I'd rather see him damned, sir! I don't propose to account for my actions to anyone."

He was really much more excited than the occasion seemed to warrant, thought Benvenuto. Mrs. Pindlebury on the other hand, appeared to be in high good humour. She was soothingly brushing some imaginary dust from her husband's shoulder, and nodding and smiling vigorously at Benvenuto.

"For goodness' sake, Pindlebury, control yourself. There's no need to shout at us because the inspector is stupid. What you want is your nightcap. Ring the bell for the steward, and I daresay Ann and Mr. Brown will have a drink, too. I think I—" She paused—"will have a cigarette."

"*Margaret!*"

Mr. Pindlebury paused, his hand on the bell. His eye-glass had fallen from his eye, and his mouth drooped open. He could not have looked more surprised if she had asked for an airgun.

"You're not ill, are you, Margaret?" he asked gently.

"Ill! Really, Pindlebury, how absurd you are at times. Just because I don't happen to have smoked before, why shouldn't I do so now? Everyone has to begin some time. Were *you* born with a cigar in your mouth, pray? Thank you so much, Mr. Brown!"

In taking a cigarette from his case she had slipped a folded note inside. She beamed at him, delighted with her subterfuge. Mr. Pindlebury had sat down and was wiping his forehead wearily.

A steward knocked and entered.

"Bring me—a double brandy and soda. What about you, Ann? Or you, Brown?"

"Thanks," said Benvenuto, "I won't have a drink. I'm going to bed. Good night, Mrs. Pindlebury—good night—Ann!"

For a moment there was, he felt, an armistice, as he held her hand.

"Good night, Mr. Pindlebury."

"Good night, young man. Sorry I lost my temper. Infernally trying, all this."

Benvenuto walked down the corridor and paused under a light. From his pocket he took his cigarette case and unfolded Mrs. Pindlebury's note. There was nothing written on it.

He stared at it for a minute, then gave an exclamation and raised the piece of paper to the light. Curled up upon the white surface were two strands of very blonde hair.

"Oh!" said Benvenuto aloud, "I see," and began to laugh.

Then he stopped, feeling suddenly foolish as he caught a pair of frightened eyes fixed upon him. In a doorway opposite a woman was standing, a grey-haired spinsterish person, wrapped in a Japanese dressing-gown trimmed with storks. In her hand she held a loofah. Suddenly she moved, the loofah dropping from her fingers, and scuttled off down the corridor.

Benvenuto picked it up and followed her. "Excuse me," he called, "you've dropped something."

But the only answer he got was a piercing scream as the woman picked up her skirts and bolted down the passage.

He was left standing there, the loofah in one hand, the strands of golden hair in the other.

THE FOURTH DAY

CHAPTER XXVI
LUNATIC AT LARGE

"Some time," thought Benvenuto Brown, "I must go for a pleasure cruise."

He was walking round the deck in the early morning sunlight, trying to persuade himself that the events of the previous night had not been simply another nightmare. It was difficult even to remember the storm with any conviction, for now the Atlantic was in a charming mood, slapping cheerfully against the sides of the great ship, anointing her with fountains of glittering spray; a vast tossing field of green-blue water seeming no more capable of mischief than a cornfield blown in the wind.

He bent over the rail, looking along the vast white side of the *Atalanta* as she cut her way so cleanly through the curling water. She was a glorious creature, imposing and efficient, a triumph of skill and ingenuity from her steel skeleton to her great salons, her theatre, her street of perfumed shops. She was calm and confident, serene and luxurious. Could anything really disturb her atmosphere of opulent ease? He straightened himself and went on briskly round the deck; the morning air was sharp and keen.

Rounding a corner he was reminded of the strange atmosphere which permeated the *Atalanta*. Facing him were two stout well-dressed American matrons, who started at his sudden appearance and instinctively clung to each other. Further on down the deck he came upon two elderly men who were laughing at some private joke; as they saw him he noticed that they both quickly re-arranged their faces; so had he seen people re-arrange their faces at a funeral.

He turned into the lounge, and here some kind of a commotion was going on; a large crowd of people all talking excitedly were collected in the doorway. Pushing his way in he

174 | ELIZABETH GILL

was surprised to find his arm clutched by a total stranger, a bearded man who blinked nervously.

"Have you heard—? He has struck again!"

"Who has struck?" inquired Benvenuto politely.

"The murderer, of course."

"Good God, you don't mean—somebody else?"

"Don't be alarmed—he did not succeed," said the stranger hollowly. "It was in the early hours of this morning—he made a murderous attack on one of the women passengers. She got away though, fortunately. I'll tell you how it happened."

He led Benvenuto to a seat, stroking his beard importantly. He was obviously enjoying himself, thought Benvenuto. The club bore type. But he turned to him with interest.

"A ghastly thing, sir. None of our women-folk are safe. I cannot understand the laxity of the authorities in allowing a dangerous lunatic on board—and what is more, allowing him, so far, to go scot free with a couple of murders to his credit. Some drastic reorganization is necessary—don't you agree with me? I intend to make a strong protest directly I land, a very strong protest."

"But what happened last night?" asked Benvenuto impatiently.

"Well, apparently this good lady," the man moved closer to him, his voice dropped confidentially, "was suffering from insomnia. A most trying complaint as I know from my own experience. She was naturally very much overwrought both by the news of the murder and by the violent storm. Some time after midnight when the storm had abated, she thought a hot bath might compose her, so, very foolhardily I thought, she ventured out to see if the bathrooms were in action again. No sooner had she emerged from her cabin than she was the victim of a violent and savage assault—and there seems no doubt from her account that her assailant was a dangerous lunatic. However, she put up a brave fight, and by some trick slipped out of his grasp and escaped. It appears that he held on to some things she was carrying, and these of course may prove a valuable clue. I persuaded her to tell the whole incident to the ship's detective, and furnish him with a description. With this sort of thing going on—"

"Excuse me," said Benvenuto, jumping to his feet, "I must go—important appointment," he added vaguely. He hurried from the room, and a few moments later was knocking at the door of the Captain's office.

Inspector Markham was alone, sitting at the desk studying some notes in front of him. He wore a pleased air.

"Ah, good morning, Mr. Brown. Any new theories to-day?"

"Good morning, Markham. I looked in to see how you were getting along."

"Not so badly, sir. In fact I may say that things are straightening themselves out. I have here," he tapped the paper before him, "a description which ought to be the means of helping us very considerably in getting our hands on the person we want."

"May I hear it?" asked Benvenuto with interest.

"Certainly, sir. It's a bit highly coloured as you might say, but the lady was in an excitable state—very natural, of course. She was attacked by this fellow early this morning."

"I heard about the attack. I'd like to hear the description."

Markham cleared his throat and commenced to read:

"'Very tall man, about six feet two. Broad shoulders. Enormously strong. Mass of fair hair, possibly a wig. Unusually long nose. Pronounced red glare in eyes. Violent manner. Noticed to be talking aloud to himself before he saw victim of his attack. Gave peals of mad laughter. Thought to have been swallowing a drug from white paper.' Sounds a bit theatrical, doesn't it, but with these facts identification ought not to be difficult. When you deduct the non-essentials, the description I have got here—"

"The description you have got there, Markham," said Benvenuto with dignity, "is a description of me, seen by artificial light through the eyes of an elderly virgin. It is true that I only stand five feet eleven in my socks, and I do not wear a wig. My nose, though well shaped, has never been considered my best feature. The red glare—"

"If this is your idea of a joke, Mr. Brown, may I remind you that I've got something more important to do than to sit here listening to your humour."

"It isn't a joke, Markham. I shall never see myself in quite the same light again. I am wounded, deeply wounded. If you'll listen for a minute I will explain the whole thing, and I will then fetch you a loofah which you may return to the lady with my card."

When he had finished Markham blew his nose disgustedly.

"Well, I did think we'd got hold of something that time. These women—show them a mouse and they'll call it an elephant if they've a mind to. No offence meant, you know," he added as an after-thought.

"I'm beyond taking offence," said Benvenuto sadly. "My nose," he stroked it tenderly, "is completely out of joint. If you've done with that description, I'd rather like to have it, Markham. It might come in useful next time I apply for a passport."

Markham looked at him suspiciously and passed the paper across to him.

"You can have it and welcome. Fat lot of good it is to *me*. Now, if you'll excuse me, Mr. Brown—"

"I will, Markham. You've got plenty of work ahead of you."

Benvenuto left him, and running down the companion-way went into the lift. A few moments later he was knocking at Morton-Blount's door.

Entering the cabin he found Morton-Blount before his mirror, tying a black tie into a large knot. He looked well but rather weak and spiritual, as though he had come through a great ordeal.

"Brown!" He turned round eagerly. "I am exceedingly glad to see you. I was about to look for you. What a ghastly, ghastly thing this is. Poor Leonard Gowling. I suppose you realize—it must have been that villain Stoke. I'm afraid there is no doubt that Gowling had approached him behind our backs."

"You jump to the same conclusion as Ann," said Benvenuto. "Unfortunately, though, I myself provide an alibi for Lord Stoke. He was with me. Look here, Blount—" Benvenuto sat down on the bed and spoke seriously. "It's no good beating about the bush. A few minutes before Gowling's death he was seen in violent altercation with someone. That someone was—yourself."

Morton-Blount sprang to his feet and faced Benvenuto.

"Brown! You don't—you *can't* think I could have had anything to do with it! To take a fellow-creature's life—" he choked. Tears had come into his eyes and he blinked violently behind his spectacles. He was very much shocked and moved.

"I understand," said Benvenuto quietly, "that you came aboard this ship for the purpose of doing that very thing."

Morton-Blount's face went slowly crimson; he fought for words.

"But—but—don't you see, don't you understand that was—is—different. Stoke is not a fellow-creature—he—he is a monster, a parasite, an enemy of the Workers. To destroy him is not an act of private vengeance—it is a duty, a duty to humanity. You *must* see the difference. You *must* realize that our motives—"

Benvenuto raised his hand wearily. "I know you see yourself as a defender of the weak, I know you're on what you think is a holy mission. What you've got to think about now is something far more important. It's only a matter of a short time, minutes probably, before Markham will come and question you. He is sure to learn from the drink steward that you went out of the bar quarrelling with Gowling last night. What happened when you got outside? Where did you go? Who did you see? Have you got an alibi?"

Morton-Blount stared at him in growing horror.

"I didn't do anything," he said miserably. "Gowling escaped from me at once, and ran away, down the deck and into a doorway. I couldn't follow him, it was too rough and I felt—frightfully unwell. I stood about on the deck for a bit—nobody was there. Then—" he passed his hand over his eyes—"yes—I know, I went into the reading-room, trying to compose myself. I was very much upset, thinking of Gowling's treachery to our cause. I tried to read the *English Review* but I felt worse and worse. Then I went down to my cabin. I was there all the time, till you found me there."

"Was there anyone else in the reading-room?"

"No." Morton-Blount shook his head despondently. "Nobody. I remember thinking at the time how pleasant the solitude would have been if only I had been feeling more myself. It was not only the storm, you know—it was the excitement, the realization of Leonard Gowling's insincerity, his treachery to his fellow-men, not only to *me*." He looked miserably at Benvenuto, seeking sympathy. But Benvenuto wasn't paying much attention to his shattered faith.

"It looks to me," he said, "as if you'd got yourself into a bit of a jam. I suppose you didn't murder Gowling by the way, from a purely impersonal point of view as towards a traitor to the cause or anything?"

Morton-Blount almost shrieked. His arms flapped up and down in his agitation, so that he resembled a distressed bird.

"You can't believe that," he said hoarsely. "You can't. I didn't—I—"

"All right," said Benvenuto. "I didn't think you did. But Inspector Markham probably will, so I suggest you run off to the reading-room and see if you can't find somebody who saw you last night. There was probably a steward on duty. And if you get into any difficulty with Markham send for me."

Somewhat to his embarrassment Morton-Blount wrung his hand.

"Thank you, brother," he said brokenly.

Benvenuto left him and went out into the sunshine. He sat down in a deck chair and stared unseeingly at the rail. He felt extraordinarily depressed at the task he knew lay in front of him.

He must see, and question, Mr. Pindlebury.

In his mind he went over and over his reconstruction of the events leading to the death of Miss Smith. He had no proof, not a shadow of proof, excepting the queer behaviour of Mr. Pindlebury, his confusion, the way he had lied about his movements on that night. It all dovetailed so neatly with the story told him by Mrs. Pindlebury. The incident of the golden hairs plucked from Mr. Pindlebury's coat was no argument one way or another. His wife obviously believed him innocent of anything but a mild form of turpitude, or she would never have told him the story of Fanny.

And if Miss Smith were Fanny—

And if Mr. Pindlebury had murdered Fanny—and if Leonard Gowling had witnessed it—or, without having witnessed it, had recognized Mr. Pindlebury as a former associate of Fanny—then the wretched little body with its drooping moustaches now lying in the ship's mortuary was accounted for, too.

Benvenuto felt more and more wretched. His eyes, staring blankly, gradually concentrated upon an immaculate pair of tan and white buckskin shoes in front of him. Idly they wandered upwards over a streamline of exquisitely cut white flannel, a purple blazer, and finally to the beautifully waved head of Rutland King. The screen lover was leaning over the rail, in earnest conversation with Lady Stoke.

Benvenuto looked at them, his eyes narrowing, the pupils dilating as they always did in moments of excitement.

The jig-saw puzzle in his mind was re-shuffling itself, the pieces rushing together in quick motion. The pattern that he had made was the right pattern—he saw it all now—but the most important piece, the key piece, had been wrongly placed. The pieces moved swiftly, each slipping into its appointed place, dovetailing. He looked at the completed picture.

Unless he were mad, it was perfect.

He started violently as he became conscious of a steward standing over him with a tray.

"The wireless operator thought you would like this at once, sir."

Benvenuto ripped open the message with fingers that shook slightly. It was from Scotland Yard.

He was not mad.

CHAPTER XXVII
THE MOMENT OF TRUTH

"COME IN! Come in! I'm delighted to see you."

Lord Stoke was more than affable. He was gushing. He did indeed, thought Benvenuto, look pleased to see him.

"To tell you the truth," went on his lordship, motioning Benvenuto into an arm-chair and seating himself opposite, "I am finding this solitude rather oppressive. On Markham's advice as you probably know, I am remaining in my suite until the end of the voyage. He felt it would be a wise precaution. After all it is no great hardship. Man is but a poor creature if he cannot find content in communing with himself."

He beamed at Benvenuto.

"I had intended sending you a note," he went on, "asking you to come and see me. I felt I owed you some sort of an apology for having unwittingly submitted you to such a terrible experience last night. That poor fellow—I owed him no friendliness, but believe me I was very much moved."

"Don't apologize," said Benvenuto, "I have had a good deal of experience of murders."

"Ah, yes, of course. Probably you are hardened. For an ordinary soft-hearted old fellow like myself it was somewhat harrowing. I am afraid I showed my feelings, made rather a fool of myself."

"As a matter of fact," said Benvenuto, "I came here to congratulate you. Of all the murderers I have ever known you are the first who has thought of using me as an alibi. Unless you keep your hands lying on the arms of that chair I shall be forced to send a bullet through the middle of your stomach. You can see where I am aiming."

Benvenuto's voice was quiet and rather gentle, but the hand holding a gun within a couple of feet of his lordship's person was perfectly steady.

A curious kind of hissing noise came from Lord Stoke's lips. He was, for the moment, incapable of speech.

"Your plan for murdering Mr. Gowling was, if I may say so, bold and ingenious. If it is any satisfaction to you to know it, it very nearly came off undetected. Last night it never occurred to me for a moment that while you were apparently fetching a letter from your cabin you were in fact shooting Mr. Gowling through the head and bundling him into his own wardrobe. I suppose you used a silencer on your gun. It was really very neat. But you have, if I may say so, an odious mind. That idea of yours of sitting in his cabin waiting for him, and grumbling because he was late for his appointment—really, I don't like it."

"You're mad," babbled his lordship suddenly. "You're stark staring mad. You don't know what you're saying. I shall have you locked up." He made a convulsive movement then stopped as the barrel of Benvenuto's gun shifted slightly.

"I am now," said Benvenuto, "covering your heart. This is a very odd situation. I have spent most of this voyage in preventing three people from shooting you. Now I am within an ace of doing it myself. I find this much pleasanter."

"Put that gun down. Put it down at once or I shall shout for help. My servant is just outside."

"That," said Benvenuto, "is exactly why you won't shout. You wouldn't like him to hear what an odious mind you've got—he might not be as self-controlled as I am. He might not be willing to let justice take its course. The lynching instinct springs up in the most unlikely people. Your servant would probably get over-excited if he heard how you had pushed a defenceless old woman overboard three nights ago, simply because she was unlucky enough to be your legal wife."

"It's a lie—a lie. I don't know what you're talking about." His face was no longer purple; it was a curious patchy yellow.

"It was bad luck for you," went on Benvenuto, "that Gowling happened to recognize her, wasn't it? She must have changed a good deal since the old days in Romley when you both knew her. It surprises me that she was recognizable at all after you'd kept her locked up in an asylum all these years. Likeness is a funny thing, the way it persists."

"Stop—stop," said Lord Stoke hoarsely. Benvenuto's quiet even voice seemed to be getting on his nerves.

"I'll explain—I'll explain everything. You're making a horrible mistake. It's true she was my wife. But I didn't kill her. She killed herself—jumped overboard before I could stop her. She was mad—she was a lunatic. Lunatics do things like that. It was nothing to do with me—nothing, I tell you. Neither was the other—I didn't kill Gowling. Blount killed him. That was it. Blount killed him. He means to kill me next. He's mad too—he's a Red, a Bolshevik."

"It's no good, Stoke. It's not a bit of good. I know all about it. I've got all the facts. You shouldn't commit your murders on board ship. You forget—it is too small a world on board

ship. There are people everywhere, watching you—eyes—
looking at you—out of the darkness—"

Benvenuto almost ceased to breathe as he looked steadily
at Lord Stoke. Then a strange thing happened. As he stared
into those small protruding eyes he saw admission, defeat
and terror; then gradually, replacing the fear, there burnt up
something else, the light of a fierce and savage triumph. Lord
Stoke stiffened in his chair and his head went up.

"You are clever," he said, "but you can't touch me. You
wouldn't dare to touch me. No one can touch me. I possess
the greatest secret man has ever known. Nobody can touch
me. The fertilizer has made me the most valuable man in
the world."

"The fertilizer won't die with you, Stoke."

"Oh yes, it will!"

Suddenly he started to laugh. He laughed so that the
whole of his vast body shook, trembled like a mountainous
jelly, and great veins stood out on his forehead. Benvenuto
was extremely glad when he stopped. His laughter seemed to
stick suddenly in his throat so that he gasped for breath, then
he looked across at Benvenuto.

"You fool!" he said. "You weak, drivelling fool! You think
that just because you've spied on me, you've got me in your
power. But you haven't, nobody has. I am beyond your power, beyond the law. I can do what I like. I can commit murder
and you can't do anything. You dare not—because the secret
of the fertilizer is here—in my head. The only other man who
knew it, the chemist who analysed it, is dead. D'you realize
what it can do? It can change the face of the earth, make
barren ground fertile—make crops grow in a day, make food
free. And it's mine, *mine*. You can't touch me. So get out!"
His voice was suddenly shrill.

Benvenuto laughed. "I wish you wouldn't be so melodramatic, Stoke. You bore me. I thought something of this kind
was probably the case. That's why I came to see you instead of

turning the evidence over to Markham. Did you think I came merely for the pleasure of a chat with you? Now suppose you listen to me for a bit. I've been thinking about this fertilizer and I've come to the conclusion that the chances are it's very nearly as important a thing as you say it is. When Gowling told me about it it sounded rather like a fairy story, but since I gather that a person as hard-boiled as yourself believes in it I've changed my mind. If it is all you suggest, it seems to me that whatever country gets hold of it first is going to be in the position of arch-bully to the rest of the world, and though I don't go about draped in a Union Jack, still I don't propose to stand by and watch any foreign country being hoisted into a position of supreme power. This is where we get down to business.

"The only person in the world, so far as I know, who possesses the knowledge that you have committed two, and possibly three, murders is—myself. And by God, if you move again I'll plug a hole through you, fertilizer or no fertilizer."

The sudden sharpness in his voice sent Stoke back into his original position, his hands lying impotently upon the arms of the chair.

"That's better. Now we can go on. You know quite enough about the law to realize that it will require your head on a charger no matter what secrets it conceals. You are simply banking on my conscience not allowing me to destroy anything so valuable. That's where you're wrong, Stoke. In my opinion this fertilizer, controlled by *you* would be a menace to civilization. That's putting it rather strongly, but I mean something very like that. The great point about you is that you're a bully—and bullies are the people who make all the trouble in the world. I think it would be infinitely preferable that the formula for the Fertilizer should die with you than that it should survive with you, and be used for your own purposes. That is what is going to happen—it is going to die with you—unless—"

Benvenuto paused, looking at the man before him. Odd things were happening to Stoke's face. He reminded Benvenuto of a bull he had once seen in Madrid, a bull facing the matador just before the drama was brought to a close by the swift downward stroke of a sword. It had been a bad bull, ferocious, yet cowardly. Everyone was glad when it was killed.

"Unless," he went on, "I come to the conclusion that the end of your disgusting life is of less importance to the world than the secret of the fertilizer. It is a nice point. It would be a pretty big responsibility for me to let you loose on the world again. There is Lady Stoke—"

"You leave my wife out of this," said Lord Stoke with sudden animation.

For the second time during that interview Benvenuto was shocked. Lord Stoke loved his wife.

"I beg your pardon," he said. For several moments he hesitated—then:

"I am willing to trade with you, Stoke. In return for the secret of the fertilizer I will keep my mouth shut. I think it extremely unlikely that anything can be proved against you without my help. I give you five minutes to decide."

The bull had been a coward. Yet, at the end, at the moment of truth, its eyes had expressed something quite unconnected with cowardice, something splendid, something that was a love of life.

"You win," said Lord Stoke. They were both silent for a minute.

"I don't see why I should believe you!" he jerked out.

Benvenuto looked at him rather sorrowfully.

"You haven't much choice, have you," he said. "But you can be easy. It's a deal."

"I can't give it to you now," said Lord Stoke, "I'll have to get papers from the Captain's safe. They're useless of course, without explanation."

"I don't want you to give it to me now," said Benvenuto. "Believe me, I don't want to carry the only other head that holds the secret. I'll come back in half an hour with Morton-Blount and Mrs. Stewart."

"I'll be ready," said Lord Stoke.

CHAPTER XXVIII
SELF DEFENCE

BENVENUTO walked slowly away from Lord Stoke's cabin, fingering the gun in his pocket. He felt extraordinarily tired. Outside on deck the sun was still shining brightly; he leant over the rail and blinked at the water. In his pocket his fingers touched a crumpled paper, and he pulled it out and read it through once more. It read:

"Person answering description discharged as cured Sept. 1st from home of Dr. Malachy Broadstairs stop name Smith stop believed formerly resident of Romley Kent stop applied for passport Sept. 6th stop no further trace—Leech."

He tore it into small fragments and watched them dance sideways over the rail, gradually downwards towards the water. Well, it hadn't been much to go on. But it had served. Luck had been with him, and against Lord Stoke he thought. If Gowling hadn't told him that Lord Stoke had come from Romley . . .

If the sight of Lady Stoke and Rutland King had not reminded him of the gap in the alibi.

If Lord Stoke hadn't swallowed his bluff.

He rumpled his hair wearily. Well, it was all right now, he supposed. The only thing that could go wrong was if Lord Stoke chose this opportunity to commit suicide and carried the secret of the fertilizer off to some other sphere. It didn't seem to matter much if he did, thought Benvenuto. The world was as it was, nothing could change it. Not even free food. If everyone ate themselves sick, he thought, they'd still go on loving and hating, killing and giving birth.

He shook himself. This was no way to think. He had got to get himself in a frame of mind in which the fertilizer was of supreme importance, a Universal Panacea, a Holy Grail. He had got to persuade Blount and Ann to change their points of view. He hadn't long in which to do it.

The League of Nations, he muttered to himself, turning into the ship. That's it, the League of Nations. Running up the staircase, he began to laugh.

When he got to Blount's cabin all amusement left him, for it was empty. With a sinking heart he knocked at Ann's door and then walked in. But it was empty, too. He stood still for a moment and swore. It hadn't struck him that there'd be difficulty in finding them. Time was getting on. It was important he knew to get back to Stoke before he changed his mind, before he had time to plot any treachery. Benvenuto had beaten him by the strength of his personality, by his will. Left to himself he might get dangerous.

Hurriedly he began a tour of the ship. It was like searching through a city, he thought irritably, as he made his way through one after the other of the public rooms. At the end of ten minutes something like panic seized him. Where was Ann—where was she—suppose she had chosen this moment to do something mad and fatal? God, that would be funny, he thought, if directly Stoke had bought his life from me Ann went and took it.

He rushed on, his eyes everywhere, his heart leaping whenever he saw a tall figure that might be Ann. He blamed himself bitterly because, for many hours, he had in a way ceased to think of Ann's resolve, he had unthinkingly concluded that the danger was, for the moment, shelved by other events.

He saw now that nothing had happened to make her swerve from her purpose. Nothing—except perhaps his duel with her over Morton-Blount; and the effect of that, if any, would be to drive her to acting alone.

Then suddenly he saw them. Standing together on a secluded part of the boat deck, talking. He raced up the companion-way and saw as he got nearer that they were arguing, apparently quarrelling.

"Listen, both of you," said Benvenuto, breathlessly. "I've got it. Your Holy Grail, your Gowling Fertilizer—it's yours to give to the world."

"How—how—what—" stammered Morton-Blount in a dazed way. Ann only looked at him with disconcerting calm.

Benvenuto sat down suddenly on a bollard. "Try to take it in, Blount, there isn't much time. Mr. Gowling, as you know, is dead. You also know who holds the secret of the fertilizer. Well, he has promised to give it to me, or rather to us. Never mind how this has come about. It should be enough for you that it has. I am going to take you down to his cabin right away, and he will place the secret in our hands. I have two conditions to make. The first is that this formula shall be given to the League of Nations."

Morton-Blount who had been following his speech in amazed delight, suddenly gaped.

"But—but that's quite impossible," he said. "The League is our enemy—Russia is not a member."

Before Benvenuto could reply Ann had taken Morton-Blount by the shoulders and turned him towards her.

"Roger," she said, "have human beings all got to be born on Russian soil before you have sympathy with them? Don't you think the rest of the world needs food? Can't you understand that Mr. Brown has got the whip-hand, and that it is a million times better that the formula should go to the League than that it should be used to benefit one particular country or one particular man? For I suppose that's the alternative—"
She turned to Benvenuto.

"That is the alternative," he agreed, watching Morton-Blount.

The Socialist looked at them desperately.

"Will you at least," he said, "agree to give it to the League with the condition that the secret is to be universally known, to be denied to no one?"

"Certainly," said Benvenuto. "Now listen again. My other condition is of course that you both give up your vendetta. You can take it, if you like, that I am getting the secret on condition that Stoke is to be unmolested."

"But of course," exclaimed Morton-Blount, with rising spirits. He felt happier now that he knew the comrades would have free food, even though it entailed the oppressors having it too. "Of course," he repeated, "all necessity for violence is at an end. We have won. Why, Ann, we need never have quarrelled. She has spent the morning trying to persuade me to back out, to leave her to act alone."

Benvenuto turned to Ann. But she was staring across the sea, staring at some fixed purpose of her own.

"My motives were not pure, like yours, Roger. Mine is a private vengeance, though I have tried to pretend it is not. I feel as I have always felt. I live for one thing. I cannot think in terms of humanity and great causes. I can only think about what I believe to be good and evil—evil—evil that has got to be stopped."

"Ann!" Morton-Blount looked at her with something like terror. There was something rather terrible in her white relentless face.

Benvenuto jumped to his feet and looked at his watch. It was almost an hour since he had left Stoke.

"I can't stop to talk to you now," he said rudely. "You've got to do what I tell you. What you do after you leave this ship is not my affair—though I can't promise not to make it so. So long as you are in this ship you are under my orders, do you understand? You are now coming down to Lord Stoke's cabin to be given the formula, both of you."

It was an odd procession that made its way down the steps, and into the ship. Benvenuto in front, walking very fast, was shaking with temper; Ann, following him meekly, showed nothing on her face but a vague amusement; while Morton-Blount bringing up the rear, blinked violently behind his spectacles and made meaningless gestures with his hands. The situation was beyond him, but at least he felt sure that he was about to become an actor in a scene which would make history and lead finally to the millennium.

The door into Lord Stoke's suite was opened by his valet.

"His lordship said would you come in, please. His lordship has not returned yet, but I am expecting him at any moment."

"Has he been here within the last half hour?" inquired Benvenuto.

"No, sir, but he mentioned he was expecting you, sir, if you would take a seat."

He moved up a chair for Ann, and went into the next room.

All three sat down and waited silently.

Morton-Blount was the first to speak. He coughed nervously once or twice and then turned to Ann.

"I don't understand your attitude at all, Ann. Surely at this moment when our goal is in sight, when we are about to become the means of conferring a wonderful gift upon humanity, all petty personal feelings should be swept away by this one fact! It is true that owing to Mr. Brown's conditions, we shall not be able to aid Sovietism as we had hoped, but—"

"Be quiet, Roger. You know that you have been deceiving yourself about me, allotting to me motives that were your own, persuading yourself that I was a heroic figure, a martyr to the cause you believe in. Don't do it any more. Try and understand what I really am. A revengeful woman, Roger, a potential criminal—not a martyr!"

Morton-Blount clasped and unclasped his hands and looked at her imploringly. "Please, Ann, please—don't go on. You do yourself a terrible injustice. I do understand your motive and I admire you for it, but you mustn't—"

His words trailed off as she turned away from him.

"You, too, Mr. Brown, you've got to listen to me." Her voice was very low and strained, her eyes wide and desperate as she faced him. "You don't understand about Lord Stoke. He—"

"He murdered your husband, or you think he did," snapped Benvenuto. He felt terribly on edge, and wanted Lord Stoke to arrive.

"How did you know? He did, it's quite true." Ann's voice was suddenly flat and weak. She leaned back in her chair, covering her face with her hands. "He was murdered because he knew too much. Perhaps you know that, too."

"Tell me," said Benvenuto gently.

"Tom—my husband—was a bio-chemist. He was working in the Sutton Baby Food Factory."

"Sir William Sutton, now Lord Stoke. Yes—go on."

"One day he told me Lord Stoke was putting him in charge of a new department. He was very mysterious about it, and said it was a great secret—something that would revolutionize human life. I was happy because he was happy. We lived in Chelsea and the factory was at Kingston. He went there every day by car. One evening—"

There was silence for a moment in the cabin, and then Ann went on:

"One evening I was waiting for him to come home. The telephone rang. Someone—the police told me he had had an accident on the arterial road. He was dead, of course."

Ann's voice was a whisper.

"The front wheel of his car had come off as he turned out of the factory. He went—down the embankment—

"He was murdered. I didn't think so then, though nobody could understand why it had happened. A mechanic said at the inquest that the wheel had been tampered with in some way, but the police didn't seem to agree with him. They said he had been driving recklessly and it was an accident. I thought so, too. I nearly died. I was very much in love with him, you know. It was the end, for me."

"And then," said Benvenuto, after a moment, "Mr. Gowling came to see you."

Ann raised her head and looked at him.

"Yes," she said. "Mr. Gowling came—and told me the whole truth. Of course he knew the motive—Tom had analysed the fertilizer. Then I knew—I had got something to do."

She said it very simply, almost smiled at him, as though now, of course, he would understand what she was going to do.

He got up and took her hands.

"Ann," he said. "You've got to go away now—go to your cabin. Blount and I will stay here. I'll come—"

But he got no further. There was a sound of voices from outside, and Lord Stoke's valet burst into the room.

"Mr. Brown—which is Mr. Brown? Come quick, sir—there's been an accident. Her ladyship is asking for you."

Benvenuto ran out of the room. In the corridor a page was waiting.

"This way, sir," he said.

Benvenuto followed him swiftly to the other side of the ship and stopped as the page knocked on the door of a private suite. He had just time to notice a card with Rutland King's name on it before the door was opened by a steward. From within came the sound of Lady Stoke's voice, pitched almost to a scream.

"You can't touch me for this! It was self defence, I tell you. He tried to kill me—he was mad with jealousy. You can't touch me, you silly—"

Benvenuto walked into the room. At first glance it appeared to be full of people. Standing in the centre of the floor was Inspector Markham, dangling in his hand a small pistol, and facing him, shaking her fists in his face was Lady Stoke, wild-eyed and frenzied, her make-up painted startlingly on her deadly pallor. Beside the bed stood Rutland King, wrapped in a purple silk dressing-gown, his romantic air destroyed by the uncontrollable trembling of his body. Next to him was a man Benvenuto took to be his business manager, a dark wizened man, whose small eyes moved restlessly around the room, and whose expression was as of one who was unable to decide if this was good publicity or not—

There was another figure in the room, but it lay upon the floor in a strangely twisted attitude. Benvenuto had no time to do more than glance at it before Lady Stoke was shaking his arm.

"You tell him—you explain to him—he doesn't understand, the bloody fool! I had to do it. It was self defence. He found me here, with Rutland. You know what he was like—"

Again she shook his arm, and now her voice changed, wheedling him.

"You're my friend, aren't you? You're the only one I've got in this ship. You know how jealous—*he* was, don't you—you saw him, the other day. You can explain to them—make them understand. They don't—here—where are you going—don't leave me. Stop—don't touch me, you damn' policeman! You're hurting me—I *won't* go with you—it was self defence I tell you! *Self Defence*—"

CHAPTER XXIX
PLEASURE AS USUAL

"THE ENGLISH really are the most extraordinary people in the world," said Benvenuto. He was sitting with the Pindleburys and addressing no one in particular. They had just finished dinner.

"After a lot of thought it has been decided to hold the farewell dance as usual to-night. But out of respect for the dead only waltzes and slow fox-trots will be played—nothing rowdy. And there will be no masks, favours, or those little things one throws. The chief steward has just told me. Pleasure as usual."

"Excellent idea," remarked Mr. Pindlebury. "It will keep the passengers' spirits up. No sense in brooding. Damnable voyage without that."

Benvenuto looked at him in amusement. He certainly didn't look as though he had found it damnable. He was drinking his brandy with a most satisfied air, and surveying the women passengers seated about the lounge in their gay frocks with the air of a connoisseur. He was obviously keeping a weather eye open for the blonde.

What a fool he had been, thought Benvenuto, not to realize that all Mr. Pindlebury's subterfuges, his testiness on being questioned, his mysterious goings on, sprang from an amorous cause. What a fool, not to realize that this ancient Casanova had spent the night of Miss Smith's death in romantic dalliance—

Then he turned to listen to Mrs. Pindlebury.

"Such an eventful voyage," she was murmuring over her knitting, "and so tragic. Though really one cannot feel very sorry about poor Lord Stoke. And I daresay his wife will not be punished. I remember something similar happening once before, a young wife shooting a jealous husband. She said it was self defence and got such a good position in some place of entertainment afterwards. Or perhaps it was in a novel. So confusing, the newspapers being so like the novels nowadays."

She changed from purl to plain, and smiled at Ann who had just come into the lounge with Morton-Blount. Ann came and sat at their table, but Morton-Blount excused himself and went out on deck.

"What a pretty dress, Ann dear. You look charming. Suppose we all go along to the ballroom, I so enjoy seeing you dance."

Ann did look charming, thought Benvenuto, walking beside her down the deck. Frail and elegant she strolled beside him, her dress falling in slender lines of palest grey. Round her shoulders was twisted a cape of the same smoky pallor, which in spite of its fragility gave her a brave and rather military air. It suits her, he thought, her cavalier's cape. But her face was calm and remote to-night, white as her pearls.

They began to dance in the crowded ballroom, a slow effortless waltz.

"The ship is strange to-night, different," she said. "This morning everyone seemed panic-stricken. But look at them now. Do you know I believe they are actually pleased at this latest—death. It's something they understand. It's conventional—a 'crime passionel.' Is that it?"

"Partly that," said Benvenuto absently. Her face was lifted to his. It was a fine tune to dance to. "Partly because to-day's sensation always blots out yesterday's. Partly because none of them know the truth, and rumour has decided to account poor Lady Stoke responsible for everything, at least until a new scapegoat is discovered. The Captain is the only man who knows the truth. I told him, this evening."

"*You* told him—? Then you know, all about everything—Miss Smith, Mr. Gowling?"

"I've known since this morning. It was luck, mostly. I expect it will all come out later."

"I won't ask questions," said Ann softly. "You are a strange person—a wonderful person—"

"That was a wonderful dance, Ann. Shall we go outside, it's very warm. It will still be summer, you know, in America."

On the deck it was warm and almost breathless, star-lit.

"Let's talk about something cheerful," he said. "We've never had time to, yet. It will be grand to get to New York. I like exploring new cities, don't you? We'll go to Harlem and dance, we'll go up the Woolworth building. We'll go to Coney Island. As a penance I shall insist on your looking at my paintings—I'm having a show, you know. You must come to the Private View in your best dress—I shall insist on that. Only then, I suppose, nobody will look at the paintings. Ann, we'll have a fine time. You've got to take a deep breath and start again—forget everything. Will you let me help? I could, you know."

"I know—you could." Suddenly she stood still, holding the rail, and put her hand on his arm. "Don't let's talk about anything beyond—to-night. Do you mind? I—I can't. I don't know where I am—I can't realize it's—over. Please forgive me."

Down the deck came a solitary figure, its head bent, hands clasped behind its back. It was Morton-Blount, wrapped in thought, oblivious to everyone. For a moment, Benvenuto thought she was going to speak to him, but she watched him go by in silence.

"Poor Roger," she said softly. "He's in mourning."

"For whom?" inquired Benvenuto. "There's—quite a choice."

"For the fertilizer, of course. He really feels it, you know. Lord Stoke dying with the secret in his brain—for Roger that is Tragedy. Oh—that fertilizer!" She put back her head and laughed. "Do you know just how much it has meant to me? I'll tell you. When Tom told me about a great discovery that would revolutionize life, I was happy—because he was happy. When Mr. Gowling told me what the discovery was—how it could change the lives of the poor, feed the hungry, make farming independent of the weather, then I was happy—because I had found a weapon against Lord Stoke. When I told Roger about it and watched his eyes blaze with fervour at the thought of free food for the proletariat—I was happy again, because I had found an ally. That is what I am like. Are you shocked?"

Benvenuto laughed. "Ann, I am relieved. I am not a missionary either. I don't worry about that, because half the people in the world are Nature's Missionaries. The other half is just as essential, for 'where's the pride in being a missionary among missionaries?' I'm not shocked because you belong to my half of the world—but I might have been shocked if you hadn't admitted it."

Ann was watching him. Gradually she began to smile, with a strange tenderness in her eyes as she looked at him.

"You are clever at saying things that make me feel good, aren't you? But you don't understand—I don't belong in either half of the world. I had something to do, but that has gone. I don't think—I exist—any more."

"I can think of something for you to do," said Benvenuto unsteadily.

When she looked at him again her eyes were wide, startled and troubled. Over her face passed a kind of bewilderment and her lips parted, trembled before she spoke. She took his hands in both her own.

But all she said was:

"I am going now. Good night."

THE FIFTH DAY

CHAPTER XXX
SKY LINE

BENVENUTO snapped the fastenings down on to his suit-case, pushed his hair into place, and went out on deck, whistling.

It was a splendid morning, very blue and sparkling, and the *Atalanta's* passengers crowded the decks in the best of spirits. They would be in dock before lunch.

The air tasted different somehow, he thought, rare, indescribable. He had an odd feeling he was about to arrive on another planet. He wondered if Ann felt that too, and wondered where she was. Finishing her packing probably.

Still thinking of her, he walked towards the forward rail. He would be glad to get her off the ship. It would be grand, taking her about New York. Grand, showing her his paintings. He would have to paint her soon. He'd like to paint her in the South of France, he thought, in the sunlight. Perhaps he could persuade her to come down to Florida. That would do her good. It would mean leaving his show, of course, leaving New York. And he had a packet of introductions to people in New York. Still, that didn't *matter*.

Why was everyone dressed for a race meeting, he wondered absently. The forward rail was lined with people, people who had binoculars slung over their travelling coats. Yes, of course, the famous sky line of New York. He had seen it on the movies.

He took a place at the rail and looked forward, then experienced a curious thrill of excitement. The pure line of the horizon which had encircled them for so long was to-day obscured by mist, but in one place there was an accent upon the vague line, as though the mist had hardened into something solid.

It was, it must be, New York. The brandishing of glasses and the excited talk on either side of him left him in no doubt; well, it wasn't very interesting yet, but soon he would see that famous sky line.

He looked about him, but there was no one he knew. He was surrounded by homing Americans, animated, talkative, straining their eyes through the sunlit mist. Probably never since the *Mayflower*, he thought grimly, have Transatlantic passengers been more anxious to get off a liner. He wouldn't be sorry himself.

Ann—Ann—Ann, he thought. Where was she? He wanted to see her walking towards him across the deck. In imagination he could see the clean, delicate way she walked, could see her wrapped in a big coat with her hair blowing sideways in the wind. He turned and looked down the decks, sure she would be there. But she was not there.

She will be excited, he thought, bending once more over the rail, when she sees America through the mist. The vague shape upon the horizon was becoming more definite now. She will smile and her eyes will grow very dark as they do when she is excited. Someone touched his arm, and he turned with a start.

But it was Morton-Blount. He looked extremely cheerful and fussily important, seemed actually less cadaverous. Possibly this was due to a large travelling coat he was wearing, and to the fact that he had put his shoulders back.

"Here you are," he said superfluously, "I can't stop—I've a great deal to attend to. I am keeping Ann in her cabin this morning, she needs a thorough rest. I can see to everything. But I felt I must spare a moment, brother, to wish you good-bye. Our acquaintance has been extremely pleasant and I trust we shall meet again in—er—happier circumstances. You must come and see me when you return—Bloomsbury Square, you know—I'm in the book. Good-bye."

His handshake was almost a grip. Suddenly he came rushing back.

"How careless of me. Ann asked me to give you this. Once more—au revoir!"

For a moment Benvenuto stood still with the envelope in his hand. Then he ripped it open. Her writing was very clear and fine, with a delicate angularity:

"I am sending you this because I do not want to say good-bye to you.

"For a long time I seem to have been living in a bad dream. Last night, when you talked to me, I woke up. And I realized that if you had not been in this ship I would, days ago, have forfeited my chance to wake up.

"It is rather a big gift you have made me. I will try not to waste it.

"I am going back to England with Roger. Then I am going to make myself a new life. Thank you for having been such a fine enemy and such a fine friend.

Good-bye,

ANN."

When he had read it he turned and began to walk into the ship towards her cabin. Then he stopped and went slowly back to the rail. He stood there a long time, his head bent, reading and re-reading her letter until the words became meaningless, became isolated shapes upon the paper.

But he knew what she had meant.

At last he lifted his head, roused by a stir amongst the people on either side of him, and looked miserably ahead. Then he caught his breath, his hand unconsciously crumpling her letter.

Beyond the bows of the ship there was, it seemed, a mirage upon the waters. The mist lay like a white scarf across the sea and rising from it, fragile and delicate, was a city of towers. Sharp and clean above the mist the towers rose in slender austerity, white as lilies in the sun.

Benvenuto closed his eyes and opened them again. Then he saw, hanging in the sky above the mirage the clumsily bulbous outline of a sausage balloon. Thank God it's real, he thought. What a city to paint—what a city! El Greco would have liked it, he thought. Fra Angelico would have liked it—he'd have used it in a background for the Holy Family.

The air was fine and keen, stimulating. The mist was thinning, blowing in thin bands across the towers. Now he could see their feet, the dark line of docks along the water front, tugs crawling along the water plumed with smoke.

What a city—

"Mr. Pindlebury tells me this is your first trip," said a delicious drawl in his ear. "Won't you take a look through these?"

It was the American blonde, handing him her glasses, her lashes fluttering at him under an enchanting hat.

As he took the glasses, Ann's letter blew away, but he didn't see it.

"I live there," went on the creamy drawl. "What d'you think of it?"

Suddenly Benvenuto began to laugh.

"I think," he said, "that it's like an ordinary town that has been treated with the Gowling Fertilizer."

THE END